The
Hunger
Desires of a
Married Man

CHARLES RUSSELL

authorHOUSE®

AuthorHouse™
1663 Liberty Drive
Bloomington, IN 47403
www.authorhouse.com
Phone: 1 (800) 839-8640

Published by AuthorHouse 07/13/2016

ISBN: 978-1-5246-1832-2 (sc)
ISBN: 978-1-5246-1831-5 (e)

Print information available on the last page.

This book is printed on acid-free paper.

Disclaimer

To my loving wife and the wives of my brothers and close friends; this story, no matter how familiar at times, has anything to do with the person you are with. However if you ever sat on my couch and received relationship counseling from me I told you that it was not for free and I'd collect one day; well today is that day. The Hunger may or may not be loosely based upon real events orchestrated by real people. With that being said enjoy this fictional tale that relates to anyone who has ever loved, lusted or took that leap of faith in that which we call marriage.

Preface

This is a revealing, informative story of relationships from a man's perspective full of betrayal, flirtation, revenge, seduction, starvation and transformation. The author will give you a peak into the intercourse of six people in different stages of courtship and the people surrounding them creating a close knit circle of friends. See how the author intertwines the characters intimately creating an atmosphere of lust, filled with intense sexual: situations, thoughts and emphasis. Out of the circle of twelve, there are four couples and six single individuals, whose paths either cross, connect, overlap, and or disconnect. Will a wife accept her husband's promiscuous ways? Will a marriage end due to lack of sex? Will two likeminded people form perfect union or is it true that opposites attract? What do you do when the attributes of your spouse which served as a criterion for selection are no longer present? What happens when a spouse gifts a spouse a free pass? This is the story of Troy and his circle of friends.

Contents

Disclaimer..v

Preface vii

The Façade.. 1

Motives 22

Paths Cross.. 34

Alterations.. 50

Quagmire.. 66

New beginnings 85

Decisions...103

Reflections 115

The Façade

Hold the elevator please! Brian looked to see if the woman that belongs to that voice was as beautiful as she sounds. After receiving his visual confirmation and being pleased with the results he extended his arm between the doors allowing the beautiful woman access to the elevator. What floor are you going to asks Brian? The woman replies: Thank you and you have already pressed it; I'm also on the third floor. By the way my name is Kim and I just moved in two weeks ago. Hello Kim my name is Brian, Brian Hillard. You are going to enjoy living in this building, all the tenants get along and we have created a loving community environment. I'm in 303 are you in condo 304 or 301 Kim. looks like we are neighbors Brian because I'm in 304. Well Kim if you need anything, anything at all let me know and if I can, I'll help. Actually Brian there is something I need help lifting; would you lend me a hand? Sure thing, no problem I don't mind helping a damsel in distress! Once in her apartment Brian's mind overflowed with thoughts of sinful lust as he was able to get a good view of her body. As she stood in her entry way removing her snow white color P coat she revealed a body closely rivaling perfection. Kim was standing at an astounding five foot eight inches tall

1

with a complexion the same color as peanut butter. Her stain washed blue jeans were affixed snug to her thighs yet struggling hard to contain her child rearing hips. Her breasts had to have been double d's and way too much for her bra to handle.

The way her big breasts were pressed intimately against one another illuminated her cleavage and had her blouse about to bust open. Her face appeared so smooth and soft and her lips were bright pink. Brian asked, so Kim what is it you need help lifting? Kim replied I'm sorry Brian I totally misled you. What I mean is that since I moved in, I have had the inconvenience turned pleasure of hearing you and you wife fuck. What, yells Brian! Yes, it is true; I have heard your wife scream your name on several occasions. Some of your sessions have been so loud that I grabbed my dildo and pretended you were doing me like you do her. Kim straddled Brian's lap and began to grind. Brian says verbally Kim I am truly flattered but I'm married and living next door to you makes an easy opportunity for my wife to catch me red handed. Meanwhile his eyes which are glued to her breasts and his mouth which is salivating forcing him to lick his lips, say you are fine and I'm ready to fulfill your desire. Reacting to his gestures Kim began to grind slowly on top of Brian trying to see what reaction he would make in return. Brian could feel the temperature rising inside his body as well as inside his pants. He tried to utter the words stop I can't but could not find the strength to do so. Kim then leant forward to initiate a kiss and with no hesitation Brian met her half way adjoining their lips to one another.

Her lips were slightly lubricated from her Mac lip gloss, yet soft, plump felling, smooth, and tasted like honey.

Her tongue rotated so gracefully inside his mouth as if it was a ballerina. His hand cupped her breasts pushing them together even further, exposing part of her left areola and extracting a seductive moan. As he continued to squeeze her breasts his fingers melted within her succulent titties. A definite hand full, Brian attempts to put her whole titty in his mouth and enjoyed every step of failure. Kim's breasts were soft and felt like jello but tasted like vanilla ice cream. They sat up independently very well despite their size and looked as if they were the breast of every man's dream. Judging from the size of her areola she has only had one child so far. Kim completely removes her blouse which was hanging together by a string connected to one button. Next she removes her bra which allowed her two friends complete unrestricted access to come out and play with Brian. Brian caressed and kissed her bosom repeatedly invoking a range of sounds out of Kim; most of which further fueled his craving for lust. Brian squeezed her breasts together until he had both of her fat sausage patty resembling nipples close enough together that he could put them in his mouth at the same time. While in his mouth he used his tongue to stimulate her nipples by twirling his tongue around the base of her nipples in a clockwise then counter clockwise motion. Every so often he gives a nipple a nibble while he keeps them completely concealed within his mouth. All this fore play has Kim so moist and wet Brian can begin to feel it through the grinding. Suddenly she stands up and begins to turn around while removing her tight blue jeans along with her cream filled panties.

All of sudden Brian realizes what is transpiring but remains helpless. With Kim standing over him, bent over with her thick flabby ass and pretty, moisturized, vanilla scented vagina in his face all he could do in response is indulge. Face first, tongue out Brian dove between Kim's ass cheeks and began to lick and taste every inch of her private parts. As he rubbed his nose against her ass and vagina his tongue stimulated and penetrated her plump freshly shaven coochy. Meanwhile Kim has managed to unfasten and open Brian's pants unleashing his massively hard man stick. Looking down onto the top of his penis she is reminded of a mushroom or a missile with a helmet on. The way the head of his penis looked was an extreme turn on for Kim and instantly made her mouth water. Releasing a huge glob of saliva Kim began to consume his dick via her mouth. The soft yet solid texture of Brian's penis felt so warm inside Kim's mouth. The way his dick pulsated in response to the movement of her tongue circling it, made her even more lustful and eager to get what she only previously imagined getting.

Finally after twenty minutes of tantalizing foreplay and seduction the moment of penetration is at hand. With Brian sitting on her chase, the naked lap dance turned into reverse cowgirl. Her ass checks press tightly against his stomach as she saddles up and begins to ride. Instantly submerged once within her warm, plump, partially shaved pussy; Brian received a dose of adrenaline and felt refreshed. Enjoying the rush of mixed feelings he tried his best to leave an everlasting impression in her as well as on her. Aroused simply by the thought of this beautiful woman approaching him for sexual pleasure due to him pleasing his wife thoroughly has his ego in the clouds; and as a result his sexual drive and confidence is fully charged. Stroke after stroke he carefully watched her facial expressions knowing that if he laid the pipe good enough that she could become a regular for him. Kim rode him as if he was a mechanical bull and she was in a contest to stay on the longest. She grinded and gyrated on top of his dick with purpose and gave Brian a run for his money. Before this moment in life Brian had never encountered a woman who could sexually stimulate him like she has done. Brian went into this encounter thinking he would turn her out and has possibly been turned out himself.

After giving Kim what she asked for and receiving an unanticipated present Brian got dressed a prepared to exit. After he was dressed and about to exit her front door he verbally confirmed that she agreed to keep what had just happen a secret from all other tenants including the landlord and especially his wife. Kim standing by the table completely naked other than her sheer silk gown using her soft and seductive voice asked Brian: are you sure you have to leave so soon? Brian opens the door then turns around to respond but upon seeing her caress her huge voluptuous breast with her sausage nipples: thick and hard, he completely lost his train of thought. Two seconds later he replied I really must go my wife will be home soon. He steps out the door and hears the elevator door chime as it opens, looking towards the elevator to his shock and discomfort he makes eye contact with his wife Lisa who's exiting the elevator.

Troy sits down in the custom made amber stained walnut chair positioned at the head of their seven foot by four foot, seventy five pound wooden table created from three oak trees that used to stand where the master bathroom is now located, he takes a sip of his coffee and releases a sigh. He takes another sip and then reaches his hand towards the pen and notepad on the table in front of him. He opens the notepad and gives a slight twist to the midnight blue gold trimmed ball point pen he acquired as a gift from his father. As a ritual he has developed, Troy gathers his thoughts over a cup of coffee most mornings and takes notes on lecture topics. As he connects the pen with the pad the ink that is captured reads as follows: What qualities must one possess to obtain a personal status of success? What characteristics must one have to obtain a social status of success? He stops writing and again takes a sip of his coffee and then reclines back and allows his mind an opportunity to organize his thoughts. He looks down at the notebook and ponders over the first thought. He repeats the question again in his mind.

What qualities must one possess to obtain a personal status of success? At one point in time if you were to ask Troy Carson to answer, the reply would be simple; a huge house, beautiful wife, four or five kids, a nice job, car, dogs and instead of the picket fence a boat. Throughout Troy's life he had managed to accomplish most of the success orientated goals he set forth. Socially he had struggled to create his own identity until the day he saw her. From his first head, to toe, to head visual inspection of her, he could feel through the tingling shivers coursing throughout his bones that she was important. She has long, full, somewhat curled hair which without a doubt looked as if she was born with it. Her face is a face worthy enough to be referenced as the image describing absolute beauty. With eyebrows hand sculptured and beautifully crafted into an arch. Her eyes, so passionate and seductive, with just one gaze inside he could clearly envision the possibilities of joy and comfort she was able to bring. Her nose, embodying perfection accompanied by the manner in which her cheeks reveal her dimples as she smiles is inexpressible. Just the mere thought of their first encounter invokes sensations that exhilarate him still.

Suddenly the coffee maker chirps alerting him to the fact that it will no longer keep the pot warm. Troy finishes his cup of coffee while adding more ideas and thoughts to the notepad. Once he was through he began to cook breakfast for his family. Cooking was one of Troy's many hidden talents and something that he actually enjoyed doing. Being a man that enjoys a hearty home cooked meal he paid close attention as a child to relatives in the kitchen. By now the time was about six o'clock and the smoked ham covered by pineapple slices that he was slowly roasting over night was cooked to prime. He turns the faucet on and proceeds to fill a pot with cold water eventually placing it on the stove. In between making the hash browns and preparing the toast and eggs Troy went to awaken the kids.

If you were to ask Troy, what in this world do you value most in life, his response would definitely be: family comes first. As for his children, he would quickly inform you that his children are his life. The moment he became a father was his most defining moment thus far in life. It was the day he decided that he would be the best man, father and when the time was right he would be the best husband anyone could ever have. Knocking on the door before he opened it and then cutting on the light Troy announces good morning son it is time to get up. After confirming his son was awake he proceeded to awake his daughter. The way Troy had the house designed allotted for the sleeping quarters to be on the same level while splitting that level into two wings, one for the kids sleeping quarters and the other for the master suite. Again he knocks before entering and announces rise and shine daddy's little princess, time to get up. Now that the kids are awake he finishes cooking breakfast.

He adds oatmeal to the now boiling water and removes the hash browns from the fire. Entering the kitchen is Samantha, his beautiful wife and the love of his life; not to mention the co-creator of two beautiful and healthy children. Good morning Troy, you have it smelling good in here this morning. Good Morning my beautiful wife replies Troy. So honey what time do you think you'll be home today asks Troy. I'm not sure, we have a big meeting today and it's rumored that someone in the office is getting promoted. If it's true we'll all probably go out after work to celebrate. Well honey, if anyone deserves a promotion it is you and I hope they can see in you what I see. But only to a certain degree! Shut up Troy you are so silly! You are the only man I want and you know that. Are you sure Samantha? What does that mean Troy? It just means that I love you and am willing to give my all to you. My all, just let me in. Troy you need to stop it, stop talking like that. Why is everything so sexual with you? I think you need some help.

As Samantha walks away Troy yells breakfast is ready and proceeded to dispense the food amongst the four plates on the table. He started eating breakfast as the rest of his family joined him at their leisure. After breakfast he took his shower and prepared for work. Meanwhile, Samantha glanced at his notepad then finished the task of assembling the children and herself before taking the children to their separate destinations. By the time she was though dropping the kids off at school and daycare it was already eight thirty. Work for Samantha was in a high-rise building in downtown Minneapolis about thirty to forty five minutes away depending on traffic. For Samantha this was one of her daily joys. The solitude she received during her daily ride to work, as well as home from work was well appreciated even treasured. For her to just have a moment of peace away from Troy and the kids, to actually be able to hear herself breathe, was refreshing. This was the time she gathered her thoughts and today his lecture question stuck in her mind. What qualities must one possess to obtain a personal status of success?

In her mind she thought that was an excellent question for Troy to ask his students. She knew that it would stimulate their minds and lead to a very interesting discussion or even some great essays. She was proud of her husband knowing he had finally found something that he was passionate about and enjoyed to do. She knew that he was more than capable and had the wisdom and knowledge to support his efforts but for a while she thought he was lost. As a matter of fact he probably would not have even had the job he currently held had she not called in a favor. Motivating and molding Troy into the man she desired has been a difficult endeavor to accomplish but she has stuck with him and had some success but slower than anticipated. When she thought of what her reply to his lecture question would be and has been in the past she began to assess her current status.

On the way to work Troy stops by the Mean Bean which is the local coffee shop and internet café right on the edge of campus that has a cigar lounge inside it. Although Troy loves his wife he has always been a flirt and had fondness for the appreciation of beautiful things especially women. At this particular coffee shop there is a very beautiful waitress by the name of Kenya who is extremely appealing to the eyes. Troy was a regular before Kenya was hired but since, he frequents the establishment more and more. While at the Mean Bean he meets up with a co-worker by the name of Tim. Tim is also a professor at University of Southern Minnesota in Minnetonka which is about eight miles west of Minneapolis. Tim's field of expertise is in Behavioral Science Analysis and Business Application. Since Troy was hired three years ago Tim Bradwell has been one of the few people he has befriended. Work is work and home is personal outside of Tim Troy keeps the two worlds separate.

Good morning Troy I see you're up to your old tricks! Tim! What is it that you mean? Troy, every time that Kenya or Daphne is working; you sit at this corner table and position yourself in a manner whereas you can keep an unobstructed view of the counter. Tim, sit yourself down and stop working all the damn time. Do you ever just live or is everything a constant analysis. Anyway there is absolutely nothing wrong with admiring beautiful women. I hear what you're saying Troy, but be careful because the seed, is the thought and flirtation is the implantation of that seed. You keep it up you're going to end up like Brian. Brian won't be here today because he almost got caught by Lisa while leaving Kim's apartment.

Wait Tim, did you say Brian almost got caught leaving his neighbor Kim's apartment. Yes Troy, Brian is jeopardizing his marriage with his constant infidelities and getting sloppy with it to be honest. As one of your best friends hear what I say Troy: stay faithful, strong willed and patient while willing to compromise in order to make your marriage work. You are truly lucky to have a beautiful wife to call your own and go home to. She has given you healthy beautiful children and you two can accomplish so much together. Alright Tim I hear you and I am listening to you and I will take it in consideration. But what I need for you to do is understand that being married doesn't mean that your eyes don't see beauty that crosses their field of vision. If you see someone that turns you on your penis won't respond just because you're involved. Tim if you were married I promise you would understand.

So time is flying today it would seem Tim, I want to get to class early today. I believe I came up with an engaging way to discuss and explore the mental need for acceptance both personally and socially. Troy will you record this discussion and lecture. Yes Tim, I think it'll be a very interesting and revealing discussion and will hopefully connect the students. All I want them to do is open their minds and pay attention to everyday things which play roles in creating the environment. By the way Tim, do you have any plans for tonight? I was thinking about going to Brian's Bar and have a few drinks. About what time are you talking about Troy? Tim I was thinking maybe around eight o'clock. Alright Troy, that sounds like a plan, if possible bring a snippet of your lecture. Troy winked his eye and waved towards Kenya as he proceeded to exit the Mean Bean. Tim watched and observed as Troy left.

Tim thought while watching Kenya blush at the gestures performed by Troy; I wonder if she knows that he has a beautiful wife and two kids already. Tim also wondered why men who were fortunate to have a woman were so often unappreciative of what they've been blessed with and always on the prowl for someone else. Why couldn't someone like him who could show a woman the value of her worth, find a life companion? Yes, he was well off financially but he wanted someone to call his own and not someone acquired for the night. Tim is a man that doesn't have a hard time attracting women but his constant behavioral analysis of the woman being courted is undesirable to the women he began relationships with.

Samantha arrives to the indoor parking garage that sits street level in her building and notices that the parking space halfway down the first row was empty. After parking in the third row she proceeded to the elevator and headed up to the eighteenth floor. Once exiting the elevator she is greeted by the secretary Felicia. Good morning Mrs. Carson; you have two messages and an eleven thirty lunch appointment with Mr. Charles. Thank you very much Felicia. After entering her office Samantha sits at her desk and thinks about the possible purpose of this previously unscheduled lunch appointment with her boss's supervisor Mr. Charles. As far as her job performance she has no fear because she does impeccable work and is diligent in her assessments and suggestions. Not to mention her numbers and statistics are high for at least the last five quarters.

As the phone on her desk rings, she answers; hello and good morning you have reached Samantha Carson Director of Marketing and Recruitment for University of Southern Minnesota. Hello Sam its Karen, are you busy? Hey Karen, girl what are you up too and when are you coming home? Funny you ask that Sam, that's actually why I'm calling; my bus arrives tonight around ten and I need somewhere to crash for tonight. Tomorrow my room at the Hotel will be available but tonight they're booked all up. Karen, you are always welcome in my home and I would be very offended if you didn't come and stay with me. That will give us a chance to catch up. So call me when the bus arrives in St. Paul and I will meet you at your stop in Minneapolis. I have to go now Karen but I will see you tonight. Alright Mrs. Samantha Carson I will give you a call you when I'm near, love you. See you later Karen and I love you as well.

When Troy makes it to work his first stop is in his office so that he can check his voicemail and see if he has any messages. Troy then calls Samantha to tell her that he loves her and hopes she has a good day as well as he hopes the rumors are true and that she is the recipient of the promotion. After talking to his wife briefly he could sense the tension in her voice. When the conversation with Samantha was over Troy decided that him and his wife needed some alone time. Troy called up his parents and arranged for the children to spend the weekend with them. Troy thought that it would be a great surprise for his wife to come home from work tonight and not have the children harassing her. Since it has been five days since his wife last allowed him to have sex with her there is a hunger building up inside of him. Troy hated feeling this way because he noticed that his will power gets weaker the more days he's forced to go without sex. With this thought in mind Troy calls the florist and orders two bouquets of flowers with the intentions of impressing the panties off his wife, literally.

After making the floral order Troy headed towards class. While leaving the Webster building which housed the offices for all the professors and deans that fall under the science umbrella he bumps into Rebecca. Rebecca White is a Chemical Reaction Specialist who heads the Chemistry Department here at USM. Rebecca was a member of the interview panel that Troy interviewed with and during that interview Troy had the opportunity to mentally undress her and got a semi erection at the images he imagined. Troy told himself that if he gets the job he would make an effort to get to know her and if something was to happen, it would just happen. In the three years that Troy has been employed he has become a good friend of Rebecca's. Although they both are involved with other people they can't deny the chemistry they have with each other. There has been so much playful flirtation with Rebecca at work Troy calls her his work wife; likewise, around the office Rebecca calls Troy her boo. Although nothing has ever happened between Troy and Rebecca the sexual tension builds with every interaction they have with one another. With Troy's will power in a weakened state this encounter should probably be avoided he thought.

Good morning Handsome says Rebecca! Good morning to you as well Rebecca you are looking stunning as usual. By the way Rebecca, whatever it is your are wearing makes you smell delicious and since you already look edible I'm not sure you want to be that tempting; it is a lot of hungry men out here that will eat you up like a biscuit then lick the plate when they are thru! Troy unless you are telling me that you are ready for a full course meal; you should keep your thoughts and your opinions to yourself, thank you! Anyway you are a happily married man Troy; aren't you? At this point in time Rebecca I am, but seasons change and rivers dry up and who knows what the future holds for any of us. Sorry Rebecca but I have to get to class; today I'm lecturing on acceptance and the reasons for our personal and social need to be accepted. Have a good lecture and discussion Mr. Carson, replied Rebecca.

Troy arrived to his classroom only ten minutes before class. He would have preferred to have arrived ten minutes earlier but the encounter with his work wife held him up. Troy has a class size of twenty to twenty eight; currently Troy has twenty four students on his roster. Typically the way Troy has his class set up is: the first ten minutes is homework collection and attendance, the next thirty minutes the students are to write about the discussion topic that is written on the board, for the next hour and twenty minutes, time is spent on discussion and lecture. As he entered the classroom he was pleased to see that so far five students were attentively waiting to be intrigued and mentally stimulated while retaining knowledge. Troy makes his way to his desk and takes out his notes and begins to write on the chalk board. Troy writes: I am Mr. Carson or Troy, June 1, 2014, and the discussion questions for today are; what qualities must one possess to obtain a personal status of success? What characteristics must one have to obtain a social status of success?

Troy enjoyed teaching his students as well as learning from them. Ironically one of the best perks of his job was one of the worst parts of Troy's job. In his class of twenty four students seventeen of them are women. As a man Troy has the tendency to mentally undress women, sometimes to visions of scary images; his x-ray vision does not discriminate. When it comes to his students, they were not exempt and he tallied that out of the seventeen, thirteen are deal-wit-able. Out of that thirteen, five could get it, and two ladies could possibly get him in serious trouble. So when the students approach his desk to announce their attendance and turn in their homework assignments, Troy can watch them approach and walk away. Troy always felt that it was okay to look as long as he didn't touch. Also Troy felt since beautiful things deserved to be admired, including women; it would be distasteful to not at least look. As much joy and satisfaction as Troy receives from lusting over these women he realizes that he could never pursue any type of relationship for multiple reasons.

Troy began role call precisely at ten o'clock on the dot and expected everyone to be professional by being present, ready to learn and in possession of any required homework due that day. Troy explained to his students that in the real world, the business world, there are: expectations, guidelines, and deadlines. Troy ran his classroom like a business as far as being very structured yet he kept the college atmosphere of the freedom to express ones thoughts, curiosities and questions. Troy announced today we start from the end of the alphabet, Thomas Whittmore; after Thomas, Sarah Washington. One by one if an assignment was due they approached his desk to turn in their assignments. This allowed Troy time to interact with each student individually and give the student counseling, constructive criticism, or congratulations depending on their grade and class participation thus far. This is one of the ways Troy was able to ensure success with his students. After taking attendance, Troy instructed the class to take five minutes to seriously consider the question. After the five minutes is complete, take the next twenty five minutes to write your answer. Remember that every individual is different, which means there is no wrong answer as long as you are truthful. When you are finished we will have someone tally up the most frequent answers.

To add to Samantha's stress and uncertainty, Samantha's boss calls Samantha into her office to have a sit down before Samantha's meeting with Mr. Charles. Samantha and her boss Mrs. Harris have always been on good terms and their relationship has always consisted of excellent communication between one another. The fact that Samantha didn't have a clue as to the purpose of either one of these meetings she was to attend today is the cause for her stress today. Good morning Erica, you requested for me. Yes! Samantha come in, please take a seat. I must say Samantha you are a superb worker, proficient in the duties you are assigned and excellent in communicating. Most impressive is your ability to facilitate the goals and intentions of USM. Samantha I am proud to inform you that management sees that your skills are over qualified for your current position and would like to promote you with a raise. Your meeting with Mr. Charles will discuss your terms and iron out the details, but you did it! I wanted to tell you sooner Samantha but it was a tight kept secret. Now that I have let the cat out the bag, go ahead and relax. Just know that I am very proud of you Samantha, you remind me of me not so long ago. As soon as Samantha made it back to her office she sent Troy a text saying she got the promotion!

After class Troy checked his messages and missed calls to notice the text from Samantha. Troy immediately contacted the florist to make one of his previous orders a delivery. He wanted to send a bouquet to Samantha's job as congratulation for her success. Troy originally arranged for the kids to be away for the weekend to secure some alone time so he and Samantha could engage in some exercise;

which is their code word they call sex. With Samantha having just got promoted, Troy figured that was more incentive to celebrate and end the night with a treat. Troy mentally prepared his self to pleasure Samantha in such a way that she'd cum way before he was ready. Troy envisioned penetrating not only Samantha's beautifully sculptured vagina but tonight he wanted to penetrate Samantha's mind and activate the emotions of her heart. He wanted to reignite the passion that they created during the honeymoon phase of their relationship. Troy had one more class to teach today but when class was over Troy went to the store and purchased some scented candles to help set the mood. Troy also picked up the flowers and used them to decorate their bed. Troy had it in his mind that maybe the reason his wife was giving him less and less sex was because he wasn't doing enough to get Samantha aroused and in the mood. Troy avoided making dinner since Samantha had plans to go out after work, instead Troy headed towards Brian's bar to order a pizza and drink. While driving to the bar Troy received a phone call from Tim. Tim explained that he had a consultant job to estimate and would not be able to attend the bar tonight. When Troy arrived at the bar it was approaching eight o'clock. Knowing Samantha gets off at six thirty and was going out with co-workers he figured she would be home around ten. After eating half of a large pizza Troy had several drinks. Troy prefers to drink top shelf Vodka with no chaser. For a little more than two hours Troy had drink after drink until he reached his limit to drive. Troy had always known when to stop drinking to prevent the distasteful symptoms of being inebriated. Troy made it home a quarter after ten and began to light the candles that were strategically placed throughout the house.

Around nine o'clock Samantha and her co-workers including Felicia ended their celebratory festivities and Erica settled the bill. Not only did Samantha receive a promotion for her excellent work, but everyone in her department also received an increase of pay due to the increase in number of enrollments. Ironically Samantha was both happy and sad at the same time. Her promotion required her to work at a different campus location. If she accepts this offer, she and Troy will be working on the same campus. Although Samantha loves Troy, work was a reprieve from Troy as well. While exiting the restaurant Samantha's phone rings; hello Karen, where are you. Hi Sam, the driver says we are ten minutes outside St. Paul. Okay Karen I will see you when you arrive, bye. Before Samantha could even open her car door the aroma of lilies attacked her nostrils resulting in the creation of a smile upon her face. When Karen's bus arrived Samantha was there awaiting her longtime friend. Hello Karen, welcome home! Hello Samantha, it sure is good to see you and great to finally be back home!

Upon entering the vehicle Karen compliments Samantha on the beautiful smelling bouquet of lilies and remarks; so I see that things with you and Troy are still good. Karen closely watched Samantha's facial expressions and body response as Samantha answered. Yes Karen, Troy and I are fine, nothing could be better! As Karen reads the card from the flowers she asks Samantha; so how often does Troy send you flowers? Samantha replies, knowing Troy it's a bribe; by the way, Karen please don't behave as if you are at work. My marriage with Troy is good. We have ups and downs like any other couple but we are in a good spot right now. I love you like a sister but we are not your patients, so please refrain from evaluating Troy and I! Samantha, you know that I love you but as a marriage counselor I can see the signs and symptoms. I don't mean to pry Samantha, but I just want you to do what is best for you; that's all! I am sorry Sam, and I will try not to pry but if you need to talk girl, you know I'm here for you. Alright enough of that Samantha, so how was your day?

Motives

When eleven o'clock arrived Troy began to wonder where Samantha was. Shortly after, Troy hears the alarm system acknowledge entry into the house by way of the garage entry point, door number seven; he began his way to intercept Samantha. As soon as Samantha and Karen enter the house through the garage the candlelit home was immediately noticed. Karen tells Sam, "looks as if someone is getting lucky tonight". This must be what you meant Samantha when you said the lilies were a bribe. As Troy opens the bedroom door and enters into the hallway he could hear Samantha say "give me a minute Karen I want to put these flowers into the dining room". Instantly Troy began to think about who Karen is and recalls those days back in college when he would pick Samantha and a co-worker Karen up from their job in the mall. Troy hears her tell Karen that she could sleep in the guestroom on the other side of the kitchen. Since Troy and the kids are probably sleeping we'll have to catch up tomorrow Karen. Help yourself to anything in the kitchen if you get hungry or thirsty. Good night Karen I'll see you in the morning. Goodnight Samantha and thank you again. Say no more Karen! There are blankets in the closet and clean towels in the bottom drawer. Karen, please make yourself at home! Samantha then went upstairs to find only Troy, naked in their bed under the covers from waist down. Troy, where are the kids and why don't you have any clothes on, asks Samantha? Samantha the kids are with granny and pops. Your flowers were my gift to you and well me lying here naked is your reward for being you; Sexy, Smart, Brilliant, Inspirational, and many other great traits that make up you. Samantha tells Troy thank you for everything baby and I love you and am so grateful to have you by my side. I am tired though Troy. I know that it's been a few days since I let you have me but can we wait until the morning? Please Troy!

Even though Troy had made arrangements and got rid of the children and had the house lit by candlelight when Samantha came home, she didn't want to have sex because she said she was tired. Samantha began to undress, which catches Troy's attention every time. Samantha pulls the hairpin from her head instantaneously allowing her long rich bodied shiny hair to drop towards her voluptuous ass. Next Samantha began to unbutton her white silk button up blouse until her white lace ruffled bra was completely exposed along with her semi sculpted stomach. Samantha unfastened the button on her black and white stripped straight leg pants. Once Samantha's pants were off and revealed her complete curvature up under her matching bra and panties set Troy's heartbeat increased rapidly and then he began to get upset. Ironically this feeling of frustration was similar to the frustration Troy experiences at work most days. Here in front of Troy is one of the most beautiful women alive and she is his, yet Troy cannot even touch her, let alone caress and pleasure her. Since Samantha is Troy's wife and the only person Troy should be sexing it infuriates Troy worst that at work. At work the frustration is minimal because Troy understands that these women are not his, so if he can't touch them it is understandable. But to have a gorgeous wife that constantly rejects your request for sex is something Troy is beginning to resent.

When Troy and Samantha's relationship first started they frequently had sex. It wasn't multiple times a day but it was at least three times a week unless aunt Flo came to visit. After their first kid, Troy and Samantha still had sex frequently. Before Troy and Samantha got married their sex life increased tremendously in quality, quantity, and overall volume. Even after their second child was born the decline in sex wasn't so dramatic that Troy began to develop a hunger for sex. Suddenly three years after marriage Samantha is full of reasons to postpone sex. Troy has always enjoyed the perk of in house pussy on demand that comes with making a woman yours and taking care of her. Samantha was no different until now which had Troy stressing trying to determine the cause. In the last year or so there had been three separate occasions where Samantha instructed Troy to leave her alone and go find someone to fuck. Samantha told Troy that his sexual appetite was insatiable and that she would not be able to provide the amount he desired. Samantha told troy that he was unreasonable and that she was more than a piece of meat, which she knows Troy loves.

Samantha has told Troy to find someone else so often he has a voice recording of her in essence giving him permission as long as she was left alone. The conversation went so far as to Samantha giving Troy what would be interpreted as guidelines. Although most men would love to be in Troy's shoes, Troy would prefer to act out all his sexual desires and fantasies on his wife. Seeing Samantha cover her tantalizing body under the blanket and curl into fetal position Troy became pissed off and could feel the resentment building up in his heart and the hunger for lust filling his stomach. Troy was upset and went downstairs to the bar in the basement to cool off. Usually this is when Troy would accept that Samantha wasn't going to feed him sexually and release the built up sexual tension manually. Tonight since he knows Samantha has company, Troy cannot even manually relieve himself, which adds to both Troy's hunger and infuriation and let us not forget his resentment.

While in the basement Troy is joined by Karen who is neither sleepy nor tired. Long time Troy hope you are treating my sister well, blurts out Karen. Troy replies with, so what brings you to town miss Karen and how is your man. Troy, I really hope you are not trying to be funny! I am in town on business but hopefully for good. As for my man Troy, since you aren't him mind your own. Troy replies, must be a touchy subject, but I'm pretty sure I know what the true answer really is. Troy, I see you are still an asshole and you need to thank God Samantha allowed you to father her children and become her husband. If you were my husband Troy I would have beat the asshole out of you. Karen, I seriously doubt that, I don't lose often, at anything. Karen I think you might have had one to many drinks; I bet you couldn't even beat me in a game of pool. I honestly think that you just like to hear yourself talk Karen. Troy! Since you feel that way pour me another shot of tequila and rack the pool table because you are about to get whipped by a woman. Say what, replies Troy. Karen, I'm about to get in your ass. There is a brief moment of silence accompanied by a slight blush and a fraction of Karen's seductive smile. That is in the pool game I mean Troy says hastily!

Inside Troy's mind he fears what might happen if he and Karen accidentally cross a boundary here in his basement tonight. He loves Samantha and would never intentionally try to hurt her especially by having sex with a close friend or relative of Samantha's. Troy quickly dismissed the thought of Karen from his mind and focused on beating her in pool. Not realizing that in the brief moment of sexual confusion between him and Karen, Karen saw Troy's penis flinch causing her to blush slightly. Karen and Samantha are good enough friends that Karen would never sleep with Samantha's man let alone husband. Karen questions whether Troy is faithful to her best friend when she personally just witnessed his penis flinch towards a woman that was not his wife. She has witnessed patients completely in denial that their spouse could be with someone else. Karen then decides to try and bait Troy into asking for sex or sexual favors. Being a very attractive woman Karen doesn't feel as if she needs to do much outside of flirts and suggestions to trap Troy and have him fall for the bait. As the game began both Troy and Karen were focused on achieving their goals. For Troy a simple victory over this pretty yet smart mouth woman who is out of her comfort zone. yet for Karen, she intended on entrapping Troy so that Samantha could be shown that the asshole she married wasn't right for her.

Karen sets up to break and instantly Troy's attention is directed toward Karen's shiny silver thong which is becoming ever more present. Over several drinks and a few games of pool, sexual tension and sexual frustration builds up forcing Troy to retire to his bedroom or cross a line not meant to be crossed. Although if Troy asked his friend Brian; what would you do if you were in my shoes? Troy already knew Brian's response would be to fuck the best friend since the wife is not willing, especially if the best friend is hot. As Troy thought about it he could hear Brian's voice, Bro hell yeah Karen is super-hot, and you need to jump on that, if not I will! Troy politely reminded himself that he is not Brian and told Karen sorry but goodnight. Troy left Karen in the basement and went to his room to sleep next to the woman he truly wanted, Samantha his wife. The next morning while sitting up in the bed Troy was extremely proud of himself for resisting the temptation of lust for Karen last night. As long as Troy has known Karen he has imagined what it would be like to be inside of her. What it would feel like to kiss her beautiful lips, both sets. Troy could remember back in his first year of college when Samantha and Karen worked together in the local mall. Troy would pick Samantha up and Samantha would ask if he could also drop Karen off at home. While dropping Samantha and Karen off Troy would discreetly stare at Karen through his rear view mirror, lusting.

But out of love and dedication to his beautiful girlfriend Troy told himself he would have to wait until he was single to ever try and pursue Karen. Besides his girlfriend Samantha was all he needed; she was smart, sexy and the sex was absolutely amazing. Troy was smart enough not to mess that up. Now looking over to his now wife and mother of his children; Troy realized he made the correct decision, or did he? Troy glances over at his beautiful, half naked wife who is less than eight inches away from him. Instantly Troy's penis begins to rise to attention; extending from a shriveled inch and a half or two, to a firm and stiff eight inches or better. Troy takes the opportunity to admire the beautiful woman that was lying directly in front of him. Troy admires the curve of her thick yet firm positioned soft cushioned booty. Then Troy takes notice of Samantha's smooth somewhat muscular arm. On to Troy's favorite part of the female anatomy, her breast; for their size they were perfect.

Troy leaned over and kissed his wife gently on the forehead then told Samantha that he loved her. Knowing how grouchy Samantha can be when first waking up. Troy decided not to pursue sex this morning. Troy did not want Samantha to make a scene, especially with Karen visiting. Troy attempted to change the subject within his mind. It upset him tremendously when he would ask Samantha for sex and the volume of her response is elevated. Troy felt betrayal and embarrassment. Troy felt if we are in the bed together and I ask you for sex discretely; why would your answer loud enough for people in the next room to hear. That is precisely why he instructed the architect to arrange the home in such a manner that the master suite was separated from the rest of the sleeping quarters. To clear his mind Troy turned the radio on in the master bathroom. Troy ran water in his personal sink and began to wash his face. After having a flashback of the way Karen's ass looked swallowing those silver colored thongs Troy decided a cold shower should cool him off. Although Troy knew that image would be a hard memory to forget let alone erase. After taking his shower and getting dressed appropriately to go fishing, Troy left his walk in closet to enter the master suite where Samantha was finally waking up on her own. Samantha asked Troy where was he going, and his reply was fishing. Samantha then apologizes for being tired last night and told Troy that she appreciated and was very grateful for the flowers he sent her as well as the whole romantic gesture of last night. Troy replied Samantha you know you are welcome and it was just a small token of what you deserve. Samantha reached for Troy and pulled him close to her. Samantha then hugged Troy and whispered in his ear; baby I love you and I promise I will give you some tonight, okay. Troy tried to hold his composure but could not hold his tongue; he told her why wait to later, let's go at it right now. Samantha said Troy now you know Karen is here and that would be rude; go fishing have fun and tell Brian I said hi. Bye Samantha, just whatever you do today just keep in mind that tonight I intend on collecting.

Watching Troy exit the master suite all Samantha could think about was how much she loved him. Samantha then began to wonder how long they could survive her change. All throughout Samantha's life sex has never made it high on her list of needs; however certain times of the month sex ranks high on her desire list. Samantha knew early in her and Troy's relationship that Troy liked sex a lot but eventually she expected it to taper off and settle down. Hearing the alarm announce door number seven now open interrupted Samantha's train of thought. Suddenly there is a knock on Samantha's door. Samantha its Karen, can I come in? Yes come on in Karen, replies Samantha. So Sam what are your plans today? That all depends on you Karen, since I haven't seen you in a whole month! How was your trip? Give me all the details Karen. Samantha the cruises were nice and the men, absolutely irresistible. Being single on a cruise ship Sam, I swear it is the best way to travel! The oceans were so clear and I saw so many fish and coral reefs. But Sam, I would have to say the best part of the cruise there was Antonio; my Latin lover. Well actually he was Belizean but Samantha if you were able to feel his chest, girl his chest was chiseled like ice cubes, which melted quickly leaving a trail leading straight to his huge man stick.

Karen are you telling me you let a stranger, someone you barley know, have his way with you! No Samantha! I lived out one of my fantasies and at the same time experienced a total and unexpected inrush of thrill and adrenaline. Samantha I truly had my way with Antonio not the other way around. Sam I instructed that man on how I desired to be touched and kissed, then without hesitation Antonio exceeded all of my expectations and showed me that he needed no instructions. Sam it was life changing, he knew his way around a woman very well. Here Sam take a look at him, I took pictures. Do you see how defined his chest is Sam. How about his package what do you think about it? Karen it looks like you two had a great time and I still can't believe that you went through with it. Samantha you only live once, so why not try to fulfill your goals as well as your fantasies. Speaking of which Sam on Monday I have an interview with a counseling firm located in St. Paul. If I get the job I will be able to afford my own condo and will actively start looking for a companion again. With the help of Antonio, Sam I truly feel that I am finally ready to move forward. I will not let David's infidelity taint and tarnish my future well-being. Oh Karen I am so proud of you cries Samantha I guess you are learning how to apply that knowledge taught to you on you! Karen in celebration of you finding your lost independence we have a date at the spa; my treat! Besides since Troy arranged for me to be childless this weekend I have freedom as well. Oh Samantha, the spa sounds like an excellent idea and the ideal location for girl talk. Both women began to snicker.

When it comes to getting a good ole delicious tasting, finger licking and tummy fulfilling breakfast; outside of Troy's kitchen there was only one other place conceivable to go. Troy and Tim both had a preference for the Pancake, Chicken and Waffle House whenever breakfast eating was the subject. It was no surprise when Troy walked into the restaurant and spotted Tim across the room placing his order with the waitress. Troy quickly asked the maître d' could he be seated with a friend if possible. Moments later the maître d' returned and escorted Troy to be seated with Tim. Troy! I should have known you'd be here, me myself can't get over the chicken and waffles, says Tim. So Tim, How was the side job yesterday afternoon asks Troy? It was alright Troy, I actually won the bid and next week will officially have two jobs. I will be part of a panel of three that evaluates new employees and clients. Troy, they need a marriage counselor, a behavioral analyst and a psychologist. Overall Troy, the company is some sort of a dating assistance company that analyzes information offered by its customers and some information solicited from external sources. Troy, not only will they pay me handsomely but I can also participate in the trials and initial launch. Tim wait, do you mean you will not only be an employee but also a member? Tim, what is the name of the company and where is it located? Ha Ha Ha Troy, I'm so excited I almost forgot; the company's name is *Companion Life*.

The best part about it Troy is that it is located just outside of downtown St. Paul. Troy, on a good day my two jobs are only fifteen minutes away from each other. Congratulations Tim, all you need now is a woman remarked Troy. Troy, you can laugh all you want, but you keep flirting with other women you might need one also, replied Tim. Troy told Tim, Thank you for your advice but my situation isn't black and white my relationship is extremely complicated. Don't get me wrong Tim, I truly love my wife and mean absolutely no disrespect to Samantha when I flirt with another woman. Of course Tim, if you are witnessing a relationship from the outside, you can never see clearly without knowing what has transpired on the inside. Troy what are you trying to say? Tim, I'll put it to you like this: if you are given permission, then it is not cheating. What Troy, even if that was true, why jeopardize your healthy relationship? Tim, let me ask you a question; if your car no longer drives but holds sentimental and collector's value, do you attempt to repair it or part with all together and get a car that functions. Better yet Tim, answer this; you buy a computer for three specific purposes: to save files, create files, review files. All other features make the computer more desirable as well as increase the value of the computer. But if the computer can no longer save or allow you to review a file then it becomes obsolete due to not being able to carry out its intended function.

So at that moment Tim you are given a choice keep the computer you invested in although it doesn't serve its function or replace the computer with a new one that will serve its function. Troy wait! What are we talking about exactly Troy, is it computers or women? Troy hastily replied both you fool, haven't you been listening. My relationship with Samantha is complicated and frustrating all at the same damn time. Tim I have been given permission to sleep with other women so long as I follow the guidelines given along with this pardon. Tim, even though I know I can and have permission to; I don't, due to the fact that the one I want is the one who is telling me to go elsewhere.

Paths Cross

Sunday afternoon Troy invited a few of Samantha and his friends over to the house for a barbeque to celebrate Samantha's promotion. Next to cooking, entertaining was something Troy enjoyed to do any chance given. Troy worked as a bartender for two years while in college and felt it would be a waste of invested time and knowledge if he didn't utilize the skills and information he obtained during that experience. For his guest's delight Troy has prepared a menu with everyone in mind. On the grill Troy has: ribs, chicken wings, salmon, brats, and hamburgers. The corn on the cob and the baked beans were also grilled while the spaghetti and breads were cooked in the kitchen. In attendance were to be the Millers, the Wilsons, Tim, Brian and Lisa Hillard, Karen, and Felicia according to Troy's invitation list. Having never left, Karen was the first to arrive and was swimming in the pool when Troy's first real guests arrived; Bob and Barb Wilson whom where Troy's neighbors to the left. Approaching the house slowly was a candy apple red Jeep Compass which eventually turned into the driveway. Briefly after parking the door opened and a shimmering golden gem covered sandal wrapped around a blemish free foot appeared. Next was a long slim leg with a chocolate colored skin tone.

Then the whole package revealed a tall sleek yet curvy woman wearing what appeared to be a red one piece jumpsuit that started from her knees gracefully hugging the curves of her thighs, hips and voluptuous ass. Not stopping at her waist the jumpsuit continues up her torso covering everything with the exception of a few well positioned cut outs and slits. Her arms were exposed from elbow down, there was a slit exposing a small section of skin on both shoulders, and a diamond shaped cutout which exposed a tempting amount of flesh in the cleavage region. By this time Samantha has come out to greet the woman. Samantha shows the woman into the house and into the backyard where she introduces her to the Wilson's, Karen and Troy. Troy and Karen this is Felicia one of my close friends from work whom I'll truly miss seeing daily, says Samantha. Felicia this is Troy my husband and Karen one of my oldest and closest friends declares Samantha. The two people playing horse shoes are our neighbors Bob and Barb Wilson. After everyone was introduced Troy whipped the ladies up some Daiquiris and pulled out a bottle of wine chilled in a bucket of ice. The ladies sat at the table on the patio and began to get acquainted making Troy nervous being its only two men around so far. To Troy's relief Tim was the next one to make it to the barbeque. Once Tim arrived Barb and Bob separated and joined the respective groups of their gender; Barb with the ladies on the patio and Bob with the men by the grill. Troy already had most of the meat cooked so upon arriving to his and Samantha's home you could eat if hungry.

Troy made a few long island iced teas for the fellas followed by a beer. Tim lite his cigar up and considered the possibility of hooking up with one of Samantha's beautiful guests. Although different heights and complexions both Karen and Felicia are nothing short of stunning perfection in Tim's eyes. Even Bob asked Troy, how do, you handle having not just a beautiful wife but one with gorgeous friends that are single. Bob stated that he and Barb would've never made it to eleven years of marriage if she had sexy friends and relatives. All three of the men began to laugh, and then continued drinking and conversing. The Millers arrived bringing along with them a bottle of champagne, a case of beer, and a portable stripper pole to be used to help facilitate drunken entertainment. Penelope and Craig Miller are the owners of three local small businesses including a beauty supply and the construction company used to build Troy and Samantha's home. Troy enjoyed playing golf with Craig as well as experiencing the cultural differences when they attend each other's events. Although never experiencing it first hand, Troy has another friend involved in an interracial relationship and knows how difficult it is to do normal stuff that most couples take for granted. Craig and Penelope met while he was stationed in Guam for the United States Navy back in 1998. After doing his time overseas Craig worked locally as a recruiter for the armed forces. At least once a month Tim, Troy, Brian and Craig go to the firing range to keep their skill levels consistent, and during the summer they engage in a lot of paintballing. Attentive as always

Bob alerted Troy to the fact that Samantha was heading towards them. Troy turned around and greeted his wife; Hey sweetie! Hmm, what are you guys up to over here, comments Samantha? Troy answers with: the same thing we always do, converse and debate! How about you women over there at the table; what are you ladies doing Troy asks Samantha. Speaking of which, Troy we need two more daiquiris and three martinis, alright honey.

You guys enjoy your cigars and man talk; I must return to my girl talk, comments Samantha. As troy walks toward the bar which separates the patio dining area from the fire and barbeque pit; Tim says: I'll give you a hand Troy. As Troy makes the drinks Tim suggests that he be the one to deliver the drinks to the ladies. What are you talking about Tim? Troy I am trying to get a little closer to the ladies to observe Karen and Felicia so I can determine if I should approach one, answers Tim. Are you sure Tim, utters Troy? Troy I feel as if it is my time with the extra job falling through and to be completely honest I'm ready to settle down and commit, states Tim. Tim to me it sounds like you are thinking with your dick and lust is clouding your judgment, responds Troy; but don't let me get in your way. Actually Tim, you and Karen will make a great couple. Troy thought to himself: Tim and Karen could psychoanalyze each other leaving them less time to interfere with his and Samantha's business. Tim inquires: do you really think so Troy? Troy hands Tim the tray with the five drinks on it, then says make sure you don't drop them.

Once near the ladies table Tim noticed that the chatter previously occurring had stopped once he approached. He stood in between Samantha and Barb and asked who had what drinks. Samantha, Barb and Karen had the martinis while Felicia and Penelope had the daiquiris. Tim notices that Karen was blushing when he handed over her martini. Tim already knew Samantha, Barb and Penelope but had only just met Karen and Felicia whose perfume was tantalizing. Tim acted like the concerned host and asked was everything to their liking and was there anything else he could do for them. In almost complete unison the ladies replied no thank you. Tim returned to the side where the men were gathered. Felicia asked who is Tim and what does he do. Penelope and Samantha began to tell Felicia the answers to her questions. Tim works at the university with Troy stated Samantha. He has no children and has never been married adds Penelope. But he is an asshole who is insecure, according to Barb whose doctor was once engaged to Tim. Samantha quickly says I don't agree with that and I have never met that Tim. Karen thought to herself: that did not look like an insecure man to me. Felicia asks: is Tim single and does he have money; I wonder what he's working with? Samantha interrupts: but Felicia I thought you were dating Ryan. Who is Ryan Karen quickly asks; with the other women waiting attentively for her response. Felicia informs them that Ryan seems as if he has something to hide and she is considering breaking up with him. Felicia says that when they are together she feels as if she's the only one for him and he gives her all his undivided attention, but when they are apart his actions are delayed as if he is with someone else and can't respond. What do you ladies think, could he be married or involved with someone else. What do I do if I find out he is and still want to be with him? Felicia iterates: he couldn't be seeing anyone else, simply because of the amount of passion he gives me while sexing. Barb interrupts Felicia and says what are you talking about? The married women all exclaimed that passion for sex is not a determining factor in whether or not your man is cheating on you. Felicia inquires for help on how to determine if she should commit any more time with this man she has, yet feels uncomfortable trusting. Penelope asks Felicia where did you and Ryan meet at, Felicia replies please don't judge me but we met at a swingers club where I worked as a topless waitress. Last year on New Year's Eve I was propositioned to join two couples in an orgy. Typically I avoided joining any of our clients in the activities they participated in while at the club. Honestly she started working there because a friend told her that, that's where all the unfaithful married men hung out; so she figured if she could see them in action she'd know who and what to avoid. I'm almost to the point where I want to become more with Ryan but something inside me is telling me it would be a mistake. So what exactly do you know about him asks Karen. Well: he is about five foot nine inches, average build, short brown hair, he drives a Porsche Cayenne and he is well dressed. Excuse me ladies, interrupts Troy, here are some shish cabob to enjoy. Samantha, Brian and Lisa should be here shortly.

As soon as Brian and Lisa arrive Brian notices the red Jeep. He instantly pawns Lisa off on Samantha and asks Troy who's Jeep. Troy responds a coworker of Samantha's why. Troy, Please tell me her name isn't Felicia. Troy replies with, "wait how did you know her name was Felicia, she isn't"? Yes it's her interrupted Brian, fuck, what the hell am I going to do; if Lisa finds out that I'm fucking Felicia, she will fuck me up and fuck up this event; Troy how the hell did she end up here, of all places. Tim told Brian he was too late because Samantha was already in the process of introducing Lisa to the rest of the women. Brian let them know that Felicia knew him as Ryan and not Brian, and hopefully if he could stay away from her he wouldn't get caught up tonight. Bob and Craig both wished Brian good luck knowing damn well that he needed it and more. Troy began to laugh and Tim could do nothing but shake his head from side to side as Brian's forehead began to sweat and he was trembling with fear and discomfort. Brian told Troy shut up! This is no laughing matter and then began pacing. I'm already in trouble from Thursday, and she is questioning everything I do. To get exposed here today would be a confirmation to all her assumptions and accusations. Tim asks Brian, how were you able to get out of that situation anyway? Brian says I'll tell you later but now I have to figure out how to get out of this situation. Troy, don't you think maybe we need to do a liquor run?

Ladies meet Lisa. Lisa this is Karen and Felicia, you already know Barb and Penelope states Samantha. Hi ladies, announces Lisa. Now that you all have met let us continue our discussion but first, what are you drinking Lisa. Samantha I'll have two of whatever you girls are drinking, I need to get drunk, replies Lisa. This weekend has been a rough one and I could use some girl time and a lot of drinks. Lisa what's wrong, what did Brian do now, asks

Penelope? Not now, I don't want to ruin Sam's party and I was trying to forget about it, answers Lisa. I don't mean to intervene but I am a marriage counselor; avoidance and denial are neither healthy, nor positive solutions for issues within a relationship, especially a marriage says Karen. I know you don't know me and I just met you but if you are a friend of Samantha's then you are a friend of mine; so I extend my professional opinion and advise to you as a friend. Thank you Karen, says Lisa. Sam, what are you all drinking? Right! We are drinking daiquiris and martinis, answers Samantha. Please have Troy bring me one of each comments Lisa. Samantha asks the other girls did they need or want anything. Samantha then proceeded to place their drink order with the bartender. Sorry for interrupting, so what were you ladies gossiping about, questions Lisa. Felicia was telling us how she questions whether her boyfriend Ryan is hiding something from her answered Barb. I'm not sure if you should listen to any advice out of my mouth today proclaims Lisa; right now I'm strongly feeling anti-man! Anti-man isn't necessarily the step either of you should take declares Penelope.

Once again Bob informs Troy of Samantha's approach towards them and the men begin to stop conversation. Troy the ladies and I need more drinks and two more glasses announces Samantha. Oh by the way Brian! Hey Samantha! Don't hi Samantha me; you should be ashamed of yourself for whatever you did to my girl. As your wife you are supposed to love, cherish, protect and shield her from pain; not be the cause of it. Troy, please bring us our drinks and the bottle of wine I sat in ice earlier. The rest of you men need to appreciate your women; women are fixtures in your life by choice, not by fate. As Samantha walks away Brian is red in the face and turns his beer upside down swallowing every last drop. Troy and Tim approach the bar and Troy begins to make the women's drinks. Meanwhile Craige lets Brian know he had better prepare an evacuation bag and sleep with both eyes open. Bob asks Craige what in the world is an evacuation bag. An evacuation bag is a duffle bag that consists of the following primary items and some secondary items depending upon the lifestyle of the individual. You need: passports, wallet, money, phone, weapon, keys, and laptop states Craige. Damn I'm fucked, cries out Brian. Craige suggests that Brian purchase Lisa an expensive hand bag or jewelry to take her mind off the indiscretion she witnessed. Or send her and her girlfriends to the spa for a weekend. Bob interjected and said that only time will heal her wounds. Craige comes back with; but the gifts will mask the pain and make the recovery time a little more manageable. Brian admits that he has a problem and can't help but to hoe. Bob said what do you mean? Brian says he can't control his desires and avoid indulging in women; it is like I have a sexual bucket list and still have more types, sizes, races, complexions, heights and situations to cross off.

While Troy mixes the martinis Tim questions him: so how do you suppose Brian stayed alive this weekend? I don't know and I don't care answers Troy; I just hope this doesn't turn into a male-bashing party because of this bullshit! Brian knows damn well he is supposed to take care of home and then this Felicia mess! Honestly Tim, he needs to let her be free to find someone who cares about her and will value her as more than a trophy. Although he's my boy, from time to time I let him know he's wrong but he's a grown man and it's his relationship. Shit, who am I to talk, my relationship isn't resistant to complications. Tim tells Troy: I can honestly say you treat Samantha way better than Brian does Lisa. Alright Tim here is your tray and I'll carry the other one. Tim and Troy approached the women's table and could immediately feel the disgust and resentment toward men that the women were giving off. Trying to not upset the women the men made minimal conversation and quickly retreated back to the safety of the pack. Once back within the vicinity of the other men Troy and Tim were able to exhale. Troy told Brian: I think you really fucked up this time, and if your mistake trickles down to me, I'm going to be highly pissed off. Let Sam not be in the mood, feeling sad for Lisa and in return I get no ass tonight after everything I've done, it is going to be trouble!

The women continue discussing the reasons why Felicia feels as if Ryan has someone else on the side. Felicia describes how just Friday night her and Ryan were supposed to get a hotel room and do dinner by the lake yet he called me around six to cancel; simply stating something has come up that needs his immediate attention. Then I heard glass breaking and a woman scream why, before the phone hung up. When I tried to call back I got no answer and then the calls started going straight to voicemail. Barb admits that the behavior described is very suspicious and the other ladies agree. Felicia adds that she has been with him before and caught him turning his phone off. When questioned about it Ryan said that the most important person in his life was right in front of him so anyone else could, should and would have to wait; he said that I was deserving of his undivided attention. At the time I heard those words I felt comfort and love but now hearing the same words in my mind makes me nauseous and uncomfortable thinking I'm not the only one he has done that to. Barb comments: it's obvious that he is cheating because you met him in a sex club with another woman; and most men don't give that lifestyle up. Penelope insists that for the right woman a man will change but only if the man is willing to. Samantha says that are still some good men left. Lisa interrupted and flat out disagreed arguing that all men are dogs and some just hide it well. Hell Felicia it sounds like your man Ryan is related to my cheating, no good and adulterous husband Brian declares Lisa. Making you feel as if you are the only woman his eyes and capable of seeing, is his specialty. Take it from me, this type of man is smart, charismatic, charming and secretly out for self, says Lisa; and don't attempt to change them. Samantha admits that it is hard work keeping a marriage together and said the secret is communication. Karen agreed and added the proper communication will alert you to the signs and symptoms of growing apart; which can happen. She stated that it is even more important in a regular relationship. To clearly define the terms and expectations as well as limits in the very beginning of a relationship is vital to the success and longevity of that relationship. I'm so confused, is he cheating or not; Felicia said I don't mean to pry but how do you know that your husband cheated on you? Karen started to answer but Lisa said: no it's alright I need to get this off my chest. Barb can you pour me a glass of that wine asked Lisa you ladies will not believe what I am about to say.

Typically on Fridays Brian gets home an hour before me. His routine is change clothes, shower and then he smokes while checking the bar's website; yet Friday was different. Sorry to interrupt but how do you know, asked Felicia. Our security system has sensors and cameras that link through the internet, answers Lisa. Every time someone enters or exits our apartment, the time and footage is recorded and saved to a database. So when I got home, I get on the elevator like normal and head up. The doors open and as I begin to step off I look down the hall and see Brian step out the new neighbors condo. At the same time he saw me, we made eye contact and he immediately went back in. Lisa, are you serious girl cries Samantha. Penelope lets her know that she knows where to bury his body. Barb opposes Penelope's statement and says talk it out first. Karen says that's not the whole story and asks Lisa to continue. Lisa reveals that her mind state was that of shock, anger and disbelief. As she walked toward this condo door where she just saw what appeared to be her husband she questioned what she actually saw; what should her response be. The condo in question was her new neighbor and she had to go pass this door to get home. Being that the neighbor whoever they are have only been living here for two weeks she had never met them. Before you know it she was at the door and had knocked on it. Sam said: you didn't! Penelope said: hell yeah I would have! Neither Karen nor Barb commented. Lisa said that when the door opened she nearly fainted, in complete shock at the situation she finds herself in. Was it Brian, said in unison by Samantha, Barb and Penelope? Lisa pours herself another glass of wine and continued.

When the door finally opened it was a beautiful woman completely naked other than her sheer silk gown, using her soft and seductive voice she asked how can I help you; please excuse my attire I was about to shower. I admit looking at her age, physique and complexion I was uneasy. I told her I was Lisa, her neighbor in condo 303 and when I saw the gentleman step out I thought I would introduce myself to you all. Hello Lisa I am Kim and it is so nice to finally meet you. Lesley would love to meet you and your husband. Is Lesley the man that stepped out earlier inquired Lisa? I thought I heard you say man earlier, would you like to come in; there is no man here, Lesley is my girlfriend but she is at work. Startled by the revelation of Lesley being a woman and at work Lisa wonders why is the aroma of sex in the air. Have you ever been with a woman Lisa? I have to admit that the walls in the condo are quite thin and we have heard you and your husband's sexual sessions. The way a man uses his tongue is incomparable to the ways a woman can utilize her tongue; if you want I could... What; shouts Penelope, Karen and Barb! No way, yells Samantha! Wow, responds Felicia. I was: shocked, upset, confused as well as I felt violated and nauseous replied Lisa. It truly felt as if I was l smack dead in the middle of a soap opera. My train of thought had long ago derailed. Suddenly I began to get shortness of breath and my face started to turn red. Kim noticed and brought me a glass of cold water then apologized for her straightforwardness. She said she assumed from the frequency of my sexual sessions that I was a freak and her and her partner would allow me into their bed if I wanted. By now I was so flabbergasted I said I have to go and exited as quickly as possible. As I was leaving she told me to think about what she said and that her door was always open for me and Brian.

It wasn't until I crossed my threshold and closed the door did I regain control of my mind. Mentally I'm trying to comprehend what all just took place from the moment the elevator door opened until the moment I closed my condo door. When I called Brian's name to tell him what just happened I received no response; which is unusual. As I walk further into the condo I don't smell any smoke and I can hear water running in the shower. I sit on the couch and try to process what is going on. I'm wondering why Brian is still showering and why hasn't he smoked yet, unless he just got home. Then the vision of him and I making eye contact as I exited the elevator flashed in my head. Was that Brian exiting Kim's door; if not than who? Why would she say she was home alone? How could he have left Kim's apartment and then get inside of ours? Is he washing away evidence? My aggression, aggravation, skepticism and jealousy levels erupted. I then went in the bedroom where he puts his dirty clothes. When I smelled them they smelled like her; like the vanilla fragrance perfume she wore. I sat on the bed and cried asking God why. When Brian finally came in the room he asked me: what is the matter. I asked him how was his day and where has he been. He lied saying his day was normal and he came straight home from work. I asked him are you sure that there is nothing you want to tell me. He leaned over to kiss me while saying: "yes he is sure" and when I smelled sex on his breathe I lost it. I tried to hit him with any and everything near me that I could lift. He ran into the bathroom for safety. When I tried to get into the bathroom he had already locked the door. While looking for my bathroom key which is kept in my jewelry box Brian knowing the danger he faced dressed as quickly as he could. As I was fidgeting with the key I heard him on his phone telling someone unfortunately he would have to cancel tonight something important has come up and he needed to address the matter. By the time I had gained entry he was off; I grabbed his phone and threw it in the toilet and flushed. He grabbed my arm and yanked me away causing me to start screaming. He quickly went into the bedroom grabbed his keys and left.

I was just paralyzed by shock, immersed in emotions and wound up ready for answers and revenge. How could he do this to me after all that I do and give to him? I poured myself a drink or two and built up the courage to get what I deserved. I realized that I needed confirmation; actual proof and evidence for me to accept it. I kept hearing Kim say my door is always open, for Brian. After four shots of Whiskey and a coke I wondered where Brian was now, I decided to find out if Brian was at Kim's house for round two. So I grabbed my purse and mace and went next door to see. Intrigued and captivated by the saga being told the women didn't notice the sun setting; or the men approaching, with the exception of Brian. Troy offered an apology to the ladies for interrupting; Craige and Bob let their wife's know that due to work they had to be leaving. Felicia told the ladies that she enjoyed their girl time and would love to have more; she exchanged numbers with the new women she had met. As everyone was heading towards their cars the moment Brian feared was at hand. Karen, Sam, Felicia and Lisa were walking out together talking. They arrived at Felicia's car first and exchanged hugs; Felicia asked Karen and Lisa did they need a ride home. Although Lisa's husband was there she wanted to show her new friend support. Karen answered no thank you I'm staying here tonight. Lisa replied I'll be okay Brian is in the car just over there parked on the street. As Felicia pulled off and passed Lisa car she got a good look at Brian who she now realizes she knows as Ryan. As she drives away in shock, her mental state embarked upon an emotional roller coaster.

Alterations

The next morning was the beginning of a new regimen for both Samantha and Karen. For Samantha today was in essence the start of a new career and life path. Tomorrow she will be working in a new office with a whole new staff to learn, teach and mold into the well-oiled machine needed to achieve the business goals set forth by the governing body. She would be the fall person if something went wrong considering she is the leader. Her intentions for today are to help Karen and check out her new office. Since the kids were with their grandparent's for the weekend they went to school and daycare from there. As for Karen her plans consisted of going to an interview and picking up the keys to her new apartment.

When Troy got up that morning he began his normal routine. He sat at the table drinking his coffee and jotting down topics and notes. The note pad today read as follows: If one can fall in love, can one fall out of love? Is it morally right or wrong to stay in a marriage when the occupants are growing apart? Is it ethically right or wrong to stay in a marriage when the occupants are growing apart? When is it socially acceptable to cut your losses and call it quits? Troy ponders and mulls over the questions so far intended for this week's classes. After the coffee pot alarm goes off Troy heads upstairs to shower and prepare for work. As usual while Troy is showering Samantha is in the kitchen getting coffee and reading over his notes. Karen comes out the guest room and joins Samantha at the table. Good morning Sam. Oh! Good morning Karen, did you sleep well? Yeah, I guess I did answers Karen. I might have had a little too much to drink last night though. I had a very awkward dream which I can only remember fragments of, but for some strange reason Troy's friend Tim was part of it. Tim, replied Samantha! What was he doing? That's the messed up part I can only remember his face being prevalent. Anyway girl; what were you reading? Oh this is Troy's notepad where he jots down notes and ideas for his classes answers Samantha. He comes up with daily topics that question the effect of humanity through psychology. For example, today's notes read as follows: If one can fall in love, can one fall out of love. Is it morally right or wrong to stay in a marriage when the occupants are growing apart? Is it ethically right or wrong to stay in a marriage when the occupants are growing apart? From this point his class will discuss the topics and then explain; when is it socially acceptable to cut your losses and call it quits? The class is learning about the need for acceptance and the psychology driving it, explains Sam.

Shortly after, Troy emerges and retrieves his notepad and favorite pen from the table. Looking very impressive with his freshly cut hair, clean shaved face, black pin stripped suite, bright white Button up and the most brilliantly colored yellow, blue, red, black and white intricately designed silk tie. The aroma of his cologne lingered through the air briefly after he walked away. He told Samantha that he loved her and hoped she had a spectacular day. He then told Karen good luck on her interview. Troy left and proceeded to the Mean Bean to meet up with Brian and Tim. Samantha asked Karen "what time is your interview and where exactly downtown is it"? It is at noon in Merriam Park West near Otis and Mississippi River Boulevard answers Karen. How far is that from your new job Sam? Samantha replied: I think it is about twenty minutes away depending on traffic. So tell me where is your apartment located? It's in St Louis Park at 31st street and Kentucky answers Karen. Besides that I'd like to treat us to breakfast today for your hospitality this weekend. Karen that will not be necessary you are always welcome in my home. Samantha get dressed I will not take no for an answer. Samantha proceeded upstairs to get dressed contemplating what she should wear today. Although it is her day off since she intends on stopping by her new job, she should be ready to make an impression; being that she is the new boss. She enters her master bedroom and then her bath suite; through the Dutch door on her side lays her walk-in closet. Although she has amassed quite a healthy wardrobe collection today she rambles through her garments unsure as if she had not anything to wear. She settled on dark blue boot cut 4th avenue pants with a color block popover blouse. As for shoes which were the most important she chose to wear her Joey Travel Two-Tone Ballet Flats. As with most women, one of Samantha's valued pleasures is shoe shopping and designer purse collecting. Today she decided to pull out her 5Jours Petite Two-Toned Shopper by Sendi. After she lay out her outfit she showered and proceeded to do her hair and make-up.

Meanwhile Karen was downstairs in the guestroom doing pretty much the same, with the exception of having to put together an outfit. She had already put together what she was wearing; in fact she bought the outfit for this specific purpose. It consisted of: Sheer-Back Wool Blazer, Silk Draped Crossover Blouse and Drawstring Wide-Leg Wool Pants. For shoes she simply wore a pair of black pointed toe pumps by Sendi. Karen's hair was already done and she wore very little make up. Karen was awaiting Samantha in the kitchen so the women could depart to have breakfast. As a matter of fact the first time they met was at breakfast when they were only girls; introduced by their parents and brought up as siblings. Their fathers were coworkers in the manufacturing business who made a small fortune investing in the stock market, then real estate. The friendship between their parents was similar to that of siblings. Over the years the same occurred between Karen and Samantha. Although after college Karen moved away, the women remained close and never lost that bond developed throughout earlier years.

Samantha, it's almost nine o'clock are you ready yet, I'm getting rather hungry yells Karen from the kitchen to upstairs. I'm on my way down now Karen, just need to transfer a few items to my purse. Upon entering the kitchen Samantha was in a state of awe looking at how absolutely beautiful, stunning and confident her best friend looks in her interview attire. Oh Karen I positively adore that outfit. With your confidence and good looks you may come off as intimidating or threatening. One thing is for certain they will most definitely be intrigued. Who are you kidding Sam it is your outfit today that wins the best looking outfit contest. I just love the way you coordinated the color pallet between the blouse, purse and shoes. Thanks girl! Are you ready? Yep Sam lets go get something to eat. Hey have you talked to Lisa today? No Karen I haven't, answers Samantha. We should see if she wants to do brunch. I feel so bad for her and knowing where all of this could lead her, makes me want to do anything possible to help mitigate her problems. Karen you have always been so sweet, that's why I love you, comments Samantha. I'll call her now she should be up and there is a nice café near her condo.

Once at the Mean Bean Troy is pleased to see that Kenya is working. Concentrating ardently on the images projected in his mind as he mentally undresses her with his eyes, Troy did not notice Brian and Tim walk in. The way he envisioned her naked was as stimulating as the first time he kissed the girl he had a crush on. Standing at a stunning five foot eight inches tall with a healthy yet athletic body type her curves perfectly positioned in all the right places. She has the meanest sexy walk ever and the way her onion booty flexes is absolutely mesmerizing. When Troy envisions her she always starts off facing him but before he's through she walks away and he watches each cheek gyrate up and down, in and out. Troy! Troy! Troy! Oh! Hey fellas how you guys doing asks Troy. Tim reply's I'm fine. Brian answers, I'm alright; so have you talked to her yet. Talked to who, asks Tim? The woman he just mentally undressed, answers Brian. Shut up both you here she comes, said Troy.

Good morning gentlemen; good morning Troy, says Kenya. Would you guys like your normal table? Yes please! And thank you so much Kenya, by the way I really like your hair, comments Troy. Awe thanks, gentlemen please follow me. Once at the table Tim started his usual nonsense scolding Troy for admiring Kenya for her beauty and body. He said, "I don't get you guys, why keep your women when you desire other women" Brian responded with that's why you can't keep a woman; you are simply too damn sensitive and sweet; not in a good way neither. Troy replied let me worry about it Tim, I have always been responsible for my actions and I do love my wife. I don't do things to hurt her and tend to not do things that I know or even think will hurt her. The fact that I am still attracted to other woman is not a reflection of the lack of love or respect for my woman; like I mentioned previously what she doesn't know won't hurt her in her mind. I agree interjected Brian. Do you know how childish you two sound, replied Tim.

But what if you are unhappy and dissatisfied and to a point where you refuse to compromise any further, ask Troy? Then you don't truly love her answers Tim. Listen Tim, it is out of Love for my wife, if I've ever crossed a line it was with no one she knew or would just happen to bump into, says Troy. There has been times when I could have and even wanted to but declined due to me knowing how it would hurt her if EVER discovered. If I ever chose to have an indiscretion with a co-worker I ensured they had just as much to lose and valued discretion highly. Out of respect for her I never let her find out any details. I never did anything in our bed or even our home. Out of love and respect for her she never once felt as if she wasn't the only one let alone the main woman. In my mind I never allowed myself to fall in love with anyone else. Look Troy, you do too much, as long as you take care of them that's proof enough of love says Brian. I disagree says Troy. That alone is not enough. I'm glad to see that you are not completely gone in the mind Troy, says Tim. As for you Brian, you are hopelessly lost my friend. Will you two change the subject here comes Kenya, comments Troy. Tim comments, she isn't your girl is she, so why change the subject. You are an idiot Tim comments Brian, a clueless idiot!

I brought you guys some coffee, Troy I put in three creams and four sugars just like you like. Thank you very much I'm certain your man is a very lucky and blessed man to have you by his side replies Troy. Why thank you Troy you are as kind as you are handsome comments Kenya. Will you guys be ordering today? No drinks will be fine we are in the middle of a debate, responds Brian. If you don't mind me asking what today's debate is concerning says Kenya. Tim replies the expressions of love and how to properly display it. No, the conversation is really, what is sufficient justification to end a relationship? If I were to ask you that question what would your response be? To me relationships are more complicated and with that being said my answer would not be so cut and paste. But most definitely I refuse to be in an abusive relationship. As long as we respect each other and communicate truthfully I believe we could overcome any obstacle or roadblock and grow into one entity that is strong enough to stand the test of time. Is this for your class? That was an absolutely astounding answer and very well merited, says Tim. I agree Tim, she is not only gorgeous but she is intellectually affluent, adds Troy; and yes, it is a possible discussion topic I might have with my advanced classes. Alright, I'll check on you gentlemen a little later Kenya says; while still blushing at Troy's compliment. Troy, why mislead women by flirting if you have no intentions of leaving your wife, asks Tim? Speaking of which does she know you are married? Oh my God Troy, we need to get Tim some pussy, a dog and a woman, comments Brian. Are there any women left that you haven't had yet Brian, replies Tim.

Look Tim, we are tired of your self-righteous, non-woman keeping ass always giving your unsolicited advice on our relationships. Chill the fuck out bro don't be a hater all your life responds Brian. Hold on now you both need to calm down interjects Troy. Tim you aren't as bad as Brian says but you could try to meddle and interfere less. As for a woman I think I know the woman for you. Who, asks Brian? Yeah who say Tim? Karen, answers Troy. Are you talking about the Karen from last night? Yep, the Karen from last night is who I think you would hit it off perfectly with. Damn Troy, I was thinking about trying to conquer her, says Brian. Wasn't she Samantha's maid of honor in your wedding; I could mark that off my hit list as a maid of honor and a counselor. Did you just say hit list, asks Tim. Come on man are you serious, you have never heard of a hit list, asks Brian. Have you never thought about the different type of women you would love to sample, or the different places you would wanted to have sex in, or how about the differences between light skinned women and dark skinned women, blonde women and red head women, black women

57

and white women, fat women and skinny women and so on. No not really replied Tim; but regardless, this one is off limits for you Brian. Troy says I second that decree. Brian tells them they are a bunch of pompous, arrogant, hating, hypocritical, assholes, but I still got love for you'll.

It was a quarter past ten when Samantha and Karen arrived at Café Plaisir where Lisa was already awaiting their arrival. Karen had not been there before and was amazed at the exterior appearance, but awed at the tantalizing aroma coming from within. This café is a replica of a French boutique with a Mediterranean inspired menu. Sam, over here called out Lisa! Lisa had acquired a booth which was in the shape of a c. not too far from the pretzel station. After sitting down the women exchange their hellos and other formalities then got down to business. First they ordered something to eat, then began to discuss the discomfort Lisa is enduring and possible motives or factors leading to her discomfort. Lisa, how long have you and Brian been married, asks Karen? Lisa replied we have been married for five years but was engaged for two and dating prior to that for a little more than a year and a half. How long have you been unhappy, asks Karen? Karen we are not in a counseling session nor are they your clients interjects Samantha.

Lisa is a good friend of mine and deserves to share what she wants without being coerced, we came to eat and talk light gossip, not a full on counseling session. I just wanted to help out, apologized Karen. I truly mean no harm and am only trying to help. Lisa stated that she would actually like to consider counseling because she feels as if Brian is completely out of control. I have never given my all to a man and yet still feel as if I'm not adequate. I do anything and everything I'm capable of to give him pleasure and keep him satisfied, yet at the end of the day I feel as if I'm nothing more than property; a trophy wife. When he is home and with me the ora is that of enduring love and devotion; yet when away I feel as if I've been demoted. I don't really know how to explain it but I feel almost as if I become a needy side chick waiting for someone else's man. How can I have two totally different men wrapped up into one? Have either one of you ever heard or experienced this type of behavior before. Karen said yes I'm familiar with the symptoms. You should talk to Felicia recommends Samantha, she is dealing with similar relationship issues. Funny you mention Felicia, responds Lisa. This morning she sent me a text asking if we could do lunch around one; she says she has something important to discuss with me. Being that we just met yesterday I'm uncertain of what information she intends on divulging. To answer your original question, I would say it has been two or three years now that I have been unhappy. As a provider he provides abundantly, as a lover he puts it down phenomenally; but as a listener and friend or confidant he is less than desirable and disrespectful. Once upon a time he wasn't like that. Nowadays he showers me with the materialistic desires of my heart, at the same time he starves my need for an emotional connection or attachment. Although I love him and would do almost anything he asks of me I'm beginning to lose my self-worth. I get so confused, he always speaks highly of me and his feelings towards me yet in reality his actions tend to differ; recently I'm just not feeling as if the love is being reciprocated. I know when I first met him it was rumored that he was a ladies man but I never experienced that man. I have always felt as if I was the only one, even around his family. I wouldn't know how to respond to find out he is cheating right up under my nose. Sorry to unleash all of my issues out onto you guys but I need to vent.

Excuse me ladies your order is ready, says the waiter? After placing the meals in front of the women the waiter asked is there anything else he could get for them. The women told him that they were fine and began to eat. After eating, it was time for Samantha and Karen to depart in order for Karen to arrive to her interview on time. As Karen reached down into her satchel to pull out her clutch Lisa said no Karen, it's all on me today! That is alright because I was treating Samantha today for her hospitality, states Karen. Unfortunately you have to pay her back some other way because this is my treat to you two women for just listening and being concerned; you have no idea how much that means to me, says Lisa fervently. Sorry Karen but I insist, this one is my treat for the both of you. Good luck on your interview Karen; maybe we girls can meet up this evening for a little while. Thanks Lisa and we'll talk later definitely said Samantha. Thank you so much said Karen, and if you want and if I can, I'll help you and Brian figure it out. I would greatly appreciate that says Lisa; we'll talk later Karen.

When Troy arrived at work today he had a lot on his mind. Good morning handsome called out Rebecca. Troy turns to speak and is awe struck. Rebecca was a temptation for the eyes on any given day but today was different. She had an ora that read goddess instead of the normal tempting eye candy. Absolutely famished for sex, Troy was no match for Rebecca today. Good morning beautiful answers Troy; I must say you look spectacular even breathe taking. If I wasn't married and we didn't work together, you would be in some serious trouble right now. Is that so, exclaims Rebecca! While waiting together for the elevator she could sense his vulnerability as if she was predator and he her prey. When the doors opened they entered into the elevator together. When the doors began to shut she asked Troy did he mean what he just said. His reply was a seductive x-ray scan from her head to toe and back up to her head followed by a hell yeah and the counter clockwise licking of the lips. She then proceeded to ask him if she could kiss him upon his lips. The thought of what she had just asked, had him intrigued. Without hesitation and before he could realize what happened, he told her I don't see why not! In the seconds that followed their lips connected for the first time, in reality. As he felt her soft tender lips touch his, he immediately became aroused. Like a predator senses the weakest prey in the herd, she sensed his arousal and extended her tongue into his mouth; as a direct reaction she then could feel a rapidly growing consolidated erection. The elevator door chime sounded alerting them to the opening of the doors. Both participants were pleased and agreed that they weren't unhappy it happened. When the elevator doors opened one by one they both walked out as if nothing had happened. Troy after Rebecca in a failed attempt to allow time for shrinkage, which watching her exit the elevator yielded the absolute opposite effect. Upon exiting, they both went their separate ways.

Thankful for his briefcase Troy hurried to his office. Troy knew when he sat down at his desk in his office, that Pandora's Box had just been opened. He sat back in his chair and recalled his interview, thinking of how he had undressed her mentally and fantasized about how her lips would feel. Now he could compare and realized her lips were softer than he had previously imagined. Suddenly he could sense the on flux of emotions rushing into his mind. He felt pride in his heart because he had just kissed a gorgeous woman who actually wanted him as much as he wanted her. Although this was a feeling absent at home and his own wife has approved coition, he felt betrayal in his spirit. The strongest of the emotions was that of lust in his mind; thinking of the window of opportunities with Rebecca that had just opened and the encounters that are in store for the future. As he licked his lips he could taste her raspberry lip gloss that was left from the earlier exchange.

A couple hours later Felicia arrived at the Café Plaisir to have brunch with Lisa. Hello Lisa how are you doing and thank you for having brunch with me today? Oh nothing to it Felicia, you seem alright and if you're a friend of Samantha's then you are a friend of mine. So Lisa, I feel that we could become good friends as well but not without trust. With that being said, I have something to tell you and I don't want to upset you but if I don't come clean it will destroy any friendship we develop in the future. What are you trying to tell me; just spit it out Felicia! Alright Lisa, but please hear me out! I think; no, I know, that the man I've been dating known as Ryan to me is actually your husband Brian. I never knew he had someone else let alone a wife. Wait! What! It can't be, interrupts Lisa. I didn't start putting the clues together until I drove away from Samantha's house and got a good look at him in the car continues Felicia. Please forgive me I truly didn't know!

So wait; are you telling me that you are dating my husband asks Lisa! Yes, well I was; I broke it off last night when I realized the truth, answers Felicia. Are you sure, asks Lisa skeptically? I'm certain responds Felicia. Did you fuck him yells Lisa? Please calm down, says Felicia. I am beyond calm and if you don't want to get fucked up answer the question! You can't tell me you're dating, my husband and expect me to be calm, cool and collected. So again, before I snap; were you fucking my husband and you had better not lie? Yes I was fucking the single man I thought was Ryan! As soon as I realized my error I broke it off; my intentions were never to be with a married man or become a home wrecker. I'm sorry Lisa but I truly just did not know! I understand if you don't want to ever see or hear from me again. I haven't told anyone else either but please know that although I knew nothing about you, I am sorry and I feel ashamed to be who I have now become! I should've picked up on the signs! I can't believe I fell for his incredible deception cries Felicia. Lisa tells Felicia thanks for the information but right now I need time to process this! Since you wanted to meet up, you can handle the bill says Lisa as she walks away!

After dropping Karen off for her interview, Samantha went to her new office on her new Campus. She wondered how often she would bump into her husband there. As promised, her contents from her previous office were delivered and IT had already set up her computer. While she was there she met quite a few of her new co-workers. According to the campus map she was three buildings away from Troy. She was able to meet her new secretary Leslie. Leslie is an intelligent, sophisticated, as well as accomplished woman; tempered, well spoken, and fluent in three languages. From the introduction Samantha could tell that Leslie would be a great friend and an instrumental component to the success of the job. Her essence seemed genuine and exuded confidence and judging by the all black dress with ear rings and necklace that match her shoes; Samantha knew that they had an awful lot in common. After unpacking a few of the items delivered from her last office she left campus to pick up Karen. Before she left, she asked Leslie to put a copy of everyone in the office's resume on her desk for evaluation and repositioning. Karen was fortunate and was offered the job on the spot. She was now a marriage advisor and consultant of a dating service known as *Companion Life*. Samantha made it back to Karen around three and Karen was eager to share her good news. Samantha lets her know how proud of her she is.

Torn to pieces by the revelation of her husband being an adulterous and deceptive mate, Lisa left the brunch utterly devastated. She felt as if she had been told she was adopted or had only a week to live. She wanted to believe that everything Felicia had just told her was lies and the whole confession was just a nightmare or a horrible trick. She went to her car and began to drive home. Although the radio was on, all she could hear were the words Felicia said to her, over and over and over until she redirected course and arrived at Brian's place of work, the Tavern. When she arrived Brian was unloading cases from his vehicle and some of his staff had come to pull it off. Brian noticed the yellow sports cars enter the parking lot driving excessively fast. He cheerfully approached the now parked vehicle next to his truck quickly; but she never rolled down the window. She gestured for him to get in the car on the passenger side. While circling the vehicle to enter the passenger side he noticed an unexpected facial expression. He entered the vehicle skeptically and cautiously mentally questioning what could she be so upset about. He sat in the car and the interrogation began.

Quagmire

Lisa is everything okay? What is wrong; have you been crying? Why is your face red? Tell me the truth Brian! The truth about what, Lisa? You can't even admit it Brian! Can you? You are absolutely right Lisa; I cannot answer you, when I know not what the HELL you are talking about! Brian besides me, who are you fucking? What yells Brian? I said, who the fuck, are you giving that dick to besides me, answers Lisa! Nobody! What the hell are you talking about, answers Brian! I don't have to sit here and listen to these false accusations, proclaims Brian! How could you, yells Lisa? So close to home; you don't even respect me! She told me everything. I can't believe you! I thought I had smelled her scent on you, now I'm certain. What and who are you talking about, yells Brian? So you are seriously going to try and deny it this time, you can't; it won't work this time cries Lisa! She told me everything; I mean everything! How could you? Look baby, I am so sorry; she came on to me and I was caught off guard! But Brian I just don't understand isn't our sex life good?

I mean, I suck your dick whenever you ask me too and even on my own sometimes. I sleep completely naked so that you always have easy access and only refuse you my vagina when I'm cycling. I dress up so you can undress me, even when I'm tired. I've pretended to be other women for you and acted out many of your fantasies even when I felt uncomfortable. I cook, clean, wash, entertain, and cater to your every need. I've given you my all and fulfilled my wifely duties copiously; yet and still you betray me and sleep with her. WHY? WHY? WHY? Am I not pretty enough? Is my pussy not good anymore? What made you want to sex her? I really need to know. Do you not love me anymore? Are you not in love with me? Brian, tell me why!

Lisa I'm so sorry! Yes I love you and am still in love with you. I only want you and of course you still are beautiful to me. So why Brian; why sleep with her asks Lisa? I swear it was a mistake; my ego got the best of me. When she told me that she hears you scream out my name when we have intercourse and wanted to experience me firsthand I was shocked and distracted. Then my ego clouded my judgment and when I realized I went too far, I left. I promise that was the one and only time I was with her. Oh my God, cries Lisa! That was you, coming out of Kim's apartment when I exited the elevator; I'm feeling sick. Baby let's not stress about this it'll never happen again like I said she was a mistake; you are the one I want, need and desire, you are my everything. Brian, please leave my car. But Lisa why and why are you crying? Brian, I truly want to believe you but I can't and I don't trust you any longer, says Lisa. I need some time to think and determine what my next move should be. But Lisa! Get out Brian! After Brian exits the vehicle Lisa rolls down the window and tells Brian thanks for letting me know from your mouth how much of an adulterous, deceitful, and promiscuous man you are. What are you talking about now woman, comments Brian. I never knew about Kim Brian, or should I say Ryan; isn't that what you told Felicia your name was. His voice went silent while his mouth dropped below his knee. The realization of his infidelities being discovered by Lisa turned Brian's face as red as a tomato. Before he could utter a response Lisa had rolled the window back up and began to pull off.

Brian got in his truck and called Craige for some advice. Craige was unable to answer his phone which prompted the voicemail to answer. Brian left a frantic and panicked message stating: Craige I am in some serious trouble with Lisa; please call me back as soon as fucking possible. For real this is urgent, I really messed up this time. Under pressure from his indiscretions done in the dark coming to the light Brian went back inside and had a double shot, twice. Next he called Troy to see what his thoughts would be. Normally he would be able to talk his way out of the trouble; but even he realized that this time was different. He knew it was a double blow given to Lisa and practically impossible to refute his own admission of guilt. How could he have been dumb enough to admit to sleeping with Kim the neighbor; when he had an inkling that she was talking about Felicia. To have to share this mishap with any man is embarrassing, yet some ideas on how to fix this blunder is precisely what he needed.

Troy's phone rang three times before he picked up. Hello Brian I'm finishing up class I'll call you back in about twenty minutes; okay Troy please call me back I think I may have went too far pleaded Brian. Okay Brian as soon as I let the class out I'll call you back. Although Brian wanted to drink this whole situation out of his mind he couldn't, due to the fact his shift starts in thirty minutes. Feeling the pressure weigh him down he laid his head on the bar. Soon he felt his phone vibrate alerting him of an incoming text message. He lifted his head and unlocked the phone to retrieve the message. The message was from Craige and read: I'll be there in about an hour and while you pour me drinks I'll listen to your problems. To prevent the compilation or complication of your drama we should speak in person.

That whole afternoon after her brunch confession to Lisa about Ryan, Felicia was sluggish and distracted. She felt relieved that she had confessed and broke it off but it was short lived; the guilt she felt for allowing herself to be compromised and put into a nasty situation like this was weighing heavily upon her. Although she was unaware of the truth, the guilt was still there. She decided to try and understand why and how to get past this and hopefully gain a new friend. She sent Karen a text asking if they could meet up professionally and discuss the relationship issues and implications that she is enduring at this moment. Shortly after sending the text it was the end of her shift and she decided to head to a local lounge located a few blocks from her apartment complex.

While reviewing the lease to her new apartment Karen received the text from Felicia. After signing the lease and accepting the keys from the landlord she checked her phone to see who had sent her a text. As she picked her phone up it began to ring. Although she didn't recognize the number she answered the phone and was delighted to find it was Lisa. The delight was short lived when she sensed the confusion, frustration, and the vengeance within Lisa's voice. Lisa said: I seriously need some help and was hoping you and Sam would allow me to vent to you again. Lisa then asked: is Samantha still with you Karen? Yes she is answered Karen. Let her know that I've been trying to call her. Karen I need you and Samantha to meet me at Samantha's house as soon as humanly possible.

Is everything okay Lisa asked Karen? Lisa started crying and said please just get here! Karen let Samantha know what was transpiring and they rushed to Samantha's house to meet with Lisa. On the way Samantha recovered her phone from the depths of her purse. She looked at the phone and noticed she had four missed calls; one from Karen, two from Lisa and one from Troy. When she checked her messages she heard Lisa say she is lost and confused and doesn't know how to handle finding out her husband and Felicia have been fucking each other these last couple of months. Wait Sam, what! Did you just say…? Yes Karen, she said that Felicia and Brian have been fucking one another for the last couple of months. I guess I know why Felicia sent me that text asking if I could offer her my help professionally.

As soon as class ended Troy hurried to his office to return Brian's call. When Brian picked up he told Troy that he got caught up with two different women at the same time and the look he saw in Lisa's face has him terrified. Brian told Troy that: Craige is on his way up to the bar to try an offer me some advice and I would appreciate if you would do the same. Although I may not do a good job displaying my affection for her, I really do love her and would be lost if she left. Don't worry Brian, I'm also on my way and we'll help you through this. Troy hung up the phone and proceeded to call his wife Samantha and let her know he wasn't coming straight home. When she picked up the first thing he noticed was the hostility within her tone. Samantha answered with the following responses: Troy what in the world is wrong with your friend? I don't know why it's so hard to keep your dick in your pants. If you ever…. As a matter of fact I think it may be time for you to make a friendship adjustment. What the hell says Troy! I know you better not let his bad habits rub off on you says Samantha. Troy in returns says I'll be home late, bye. Samantha says umm hmm and they ended the phone call with one another. Troy, now a little irritated, heads to Brian's bar to converse and clear his mind. Like a devil in a dress, in his moment of agitation comes Rebecca in a pinstripe business suit looking as attractive as a million dollars.

Craige arrived at the Tavern first and although Brian was there at work; he could clearly see that Brian was more focused on his marital issues rather than his bartending duties. The highly flirtatious, suave, woman idolizing Brian was absent; exposing the more vulnerable, insecure, uncertain kid I met in Jr. High thinks Craige. Hey! Bry! So what's the big emergency? Did you buy the damn hand bag like I suggested? Damn man, Craige I think I really fucked up this time, says Brian. Yes I bought her a bag and a bracelet. Everything was cool when she woke up and found it. She sent me a thank you text and told me how she wanted to get kinky with me tonight. She said she apologized for accusing me of something I didn't do. She said she must have been missing me so much that she pictured me by the neighbor's apartment door. She made me promise I would allow her to feel my warm semen drip down her face tonight during foreplay. She said that she had made a special design for me with her hair down there but completely removed the surrounding forest. Brian I don't want to hear intimates about your wife; a mistress is one thing a wife is totally another, interrupts Craige. Craige, just listen replies Brian. So as the day goes by I'm thinking cool I'll get some flowers, go home, sexually put it down on her like it was the first time and I had something to prove, then seal the deal with the 14 karat gold bracelet inscribed: the only woman for me- Brian.

So when I saw her car come flying into the parking lot earlier I was a bit thrown off. I mean to be honest I thought maybe she couldn't wait until tonight and wanted to get some dick immediately; boy was I wrong. Hey guys what did I miss says Troy as he approaches the end of the bar where Brian and Craige are conversing. Brian responds just sit and listen while I fill you both in. So Troy, I bought Lisa a make-up bag since she's been upset over spotting me or thinking she spotted me coming out of the neighbor's house. Wait! Did you say she thinks she saw me, asked Craige? Yes since she had no proof I convinced her that It simply wasn't me and whatever explanations she came up with I supported;

as long as it didn't implicate me. So everything was repaired when I left this morning and I was going to reinforce it with a bracelet. So when she came up here earlier to confront me I wasn't prepared. I approached her car and she just gestured for me to get in the passenger seat. That is when I looked at her facial expression through the windshield and realized she was upset about something; even then I didn't think it was me or something I did. What did, you think she was mad about Brian asked Troy? Seriously Troy, I figured it was something petty that she needed reassurance about or some other woman stuff, answers Brian.

So I sit in the car and she is like: Tell me the truth Brian. I'm like the truth about what. She say you lying, who you fucking? I'm like what, nobody. She tells me I might as well be honest because she knows I'm screwing someone else. I say I'm not and because I'm not, I'm not going to take these false accusations. She start crying talking about how could you and why so close to home and some other shit. Now I'm getting frustrated so I'm like look I told you before that it wasn't me. She interrupts me saying she told me everything. I'm getting nervous but standing firm that it wasn't me; but when I looked into her eyes I could see the heartache and pain I caused her. She started asking me was she ugly, was her pussy not good enough, and all sorts of other insecure statements and suggestions for why it was somehow because of her inadequacies. I wasn't cruel enough to continue my story so I owned up to my mistake. You did what, yells Craige! I was caught so I confessed, answers Brian. Troy interjected but Brian so far there is only circumstantial evidence. But Troy, the look in her eyes said you are caught red handed and disappointing me further by your constant denial says Brian.

So I explained to Lisa that it wasn't her at all and I truly love her but had made a mistake during a moment of weakness. I explained that my ego was so inflated when she told me that she hears you scream out my name when we have intercourse and wanted to experience me firsthand; I was shocked, distracted and a mistake was made. WOW, says Troy! Awe Damn, says Craige! That isn't even the worst part, exclaims Brian. I fucking confessed to the wrong indiscretion. You did what, yells both Troy and Craige. I thought she was talking about Kim; being so close to home and all. Fucking moron shouts Craige! Give him a break replies Troy. He made a mistake, a costly one but a mistake none the less; now I know what Sam was upset about. But let me guess Brian, she was talking about Felicia. Yeah it was Felicia, Lisa never said a name but since she had already suspected me of being with the neighbor, I just assumed it was the neighbor Kim who had confessed to her, proclaims Brian. I know I fucked up really bad but; is there any way to repair or mend the relationship? Can I somehow sweep this under the rug, and what will it cost? Please fellas tell me, is this the end of our chapter or can we add more to our story?

Due to the strained emotion and stress heard in Lisa's voice Karen and Sam rushed to Sam's house to meet Lisa who was already there awaiting their arrival. Sam placed an order to Ristorante Luigi on the way home and arranged for it to be delivered to her home about twenty minutes after they made it home. As previously stated Lisa was in

Sam's driveway sitting in her car crying when Karen and Sam pulled up. Immediately Samantha ran to Lisa and apologized for what happened and for introducing her to Felicia. Samantha felt very guilty but promised Lisa that she had no prior knowledge that Felicia and Brian knew each other; let alone that they were sexually or romantically involved. Lisa said I know Sam, Felicia explained that you had no part of what transpired. Excuse me Lisa but how exactly did she come clean asked Karen while taking notes in her notepad. Felicia arrived at the café sat down and thanked me for meeting with her. We exchanged pleasantries, and then I pretty much asked what the reason is for this brunch. Felicia replies: I feel that we could become good friends but not without trust. With that being said, I have something to tell you Lisa and I don't want to upset you but if I don't come clean it will destroy any friendship we develop in the future. I then said impatiently: what are you trying to tell me; just spit it out Felicia. Alright Lisa, the man that I've been dating known as Ryan to me, is actually your husband Brian. What, yells Samantha! Are you serious? I said the same thing comments Lisa. So I ask Felicia: are you telling me that you are dating my husband. Yes, well I was; I broke it off last night when I realized the truth, answers Felicia. I didn't start putting the clues together until I drove away from Samantha's house and got a good look at him in the car continues Felicia. Please forgive me I truly didn't know. By this point I'm frustrated, pissed off, and engulfed with emotions and I ask Felicia are you fucking him? Please calm down, says Felicia. Lisa replies, I am beyond calm and if you don't want to get fucked up answer the question! You can't tell me you're dating, my husband and expect me to be calm, cool and collected. So again, before I snap; were you fucking my husband and you had better not lie? Yes answers Felicia, I was fucking the single man I thought was Ryan. As soon as I realized my error I broke it off; my intentions were never to be with a married man or become a home wrecker. How did she tell you about it, asked Karen.

Lisa said that Felicia was nice about it and didn't seem like she enjoyed telling me about my husband. She swears that she never knew he had a woman let alone a wife. She apologized but felt she had to come clean because she was also hurting. She said that she didn't want to spread our business so I was the only one she had told so far but she needed to talk to someone else to help get clarity. I never wanted to believe her but I knew deep down she was telling the truth. Aggravated and infuriated I told her to pay the bill and I left. While on my way home I could hear Felicia's words replay over and over again and again inside my head until I redirected my course to Brian's work place. Once there, I confronted my so called husband and was hurt even more than before. Girl it is going to be alright, we are here for you girl, says Samantha.

Out of the three years we have been married and the two prior years of courtship I have never felt this unappreciated and insecure. With all of the things we've experienced through our short but eventful existence I never imagined Brian could make me feel so low and depressed. My friends used to say he wasn't good enough for me or that he only wants me because of my social prowess. Even his brother tried to tell me discretely that he only wanted to make me his trophy. A trophy wife, comments Karen. Yes, that is precisely what he said I would become answers Lisa. I didn't believe it then although I'm starting to believe it now. Today has been so completely fucking horrific I don't want to believe it. I don't know rather to get out or get even. Or better yet maybe I should just kill the two- timing, rather three-timing bastard. Wait Lisa, I know Brian isn't always the best husband but I don't think you really want to kill the man, comments Samantha.

What do you mean Lisa when you say he is a three-timing bastard, inquires Karen. Lisa breaks down and begins sobbing and crying hysterically and confesses that she must be a horrible wife who is no longer desirable. Don't say that Lisa, you know that's not true, declares Samantha. Yes Sam I agree, Lisa you have to be strong and secure because you are indeed a beautiful woman on the outside as well as the inside. Understand your worth and that in life you will have to make compromises but never compromise what you are worth, encourages Karen. Today I found out my previous suspicions were true; not only did he cheat on me with Felicia but he also reveals from his mouth that he fucked the neighbor. My fucking neighbor screams Lisa! He put his cock inside our fucking neighbor cries Lisa! Both Samantha and Karen embrace Lisa with Hugs and kisses of sympathy, love, affection and support. Drunken with emotion Lisa is completely overwhelmed and starts to shut down.

Before you know it the time was approaching eight thirty in the evening and Penelope was calling her husband to see why he hadn't come home for dinner. Craige had only planned on staying for a couple of hours but according to his watch he had been there twice as long as intended. He answered the phone while heading towards an exit with intent to damper the background noises. After being outside for a few minutes Craige returned and announced his departure for the evening. Troy also decided it was time to go home; although he was a bit saddened by the lack of a call from his significant other. Brian only had a couple of hours left in his shift in which he decided he should actually work since most of the night he was getting counseled. Upset with his closest friends for their candor; he couldn't believe they didn't side with him.

Brian grasped with accepting the knowledge he had learned today. It was revealed that he has no legitimate reason at all to step out on his wife, especially when Lisa is as good of a woman as she is. Not only is he selfish but also immature pertaining especially to his hit list. It was advised that he give up either his aspirations to complete his hit list extensively or allow his good woman, excellent wife, and sexually generous companion to find someone worthy of her. Or risk turning her into an evil scorned woman. Brian was both perplexed and perturbed at the notion that his closest friends wanted his wife for themselves just would not leave his mind. Although they both are involved with their own women and out of the group, he is the promiscuous one, he still had jealous thoughts that he felt were hidden motives as to the responses from his friends. He was forced to contemplate whether or not the way he treated Lisa matched the way he felt. Brian considered if his Love for Lisa showed in his everyday actions.

Troy called Samantha when he got inside his car to let her know he was heading home, but only received her voicemail. When he arrived home he noticed Lisa's car in the driveway. As soon as he exited his vehicle in the garage he could hear chatter from within the house. Having just left Brian, he pretty much knew what the topic of the ladies discussion was. He decided it was probably in his best interest to avoid the ladies. Although the women didn't see him come in the alarm alerted them of his presence. Karen looked at her watch and announced that it was a quarter after nine and she had to start her new job in the morning. Samantha agreed and stated the same. Lisa decided that she should be going home but Samantha insisted she stay for the night. Samantha suggested she go to sleep and allow her mind time to process the transgressions against her. Karen agreed adding that major life changing decisions should never be made while in a heightened emotional state.

Although Lisa tried to go to sleep, her mind flatly refused; she simply couldn't not stop thinking and questioning the reasons and motives for this cardinal betrayal. What could she have done to prevent this adultery from happening? She felt guilty but realized that she hadn't been the one who stepped out on the relationship; it was the other way around. She started too serious assess herself in an effort to determine and identify her own personal worth. Just as one of her friends suggested, she determined that she didn't deserve to be treated the way Brian treats her, and that she deserved better. Suddenly her phone rings and she ignores it knowing from the ringtone played that it was her husband, soon to be ex-husband. After sending seven calls to the voicemail she decided to power off the phone in an attempt to silence Brian and get some sleep. While attempting to shut down the phone she received a text from Brian reading: I'm so sorry! I love you. It only offended and infuriated her.

She thought to herself, how dare he say he loves me and is fucking the world while carrying on other relationships using various aliases. I don't know what I did to deserve this abuse, mistreatment, and flat out deceit. I feel as if I don't know the man I love and thought I married. The warnings and rumors might have held merit. How will I proceed from this point on? Should I dismiss his infidelity and stand by my man? Or should I get even and do what he did to me to him so he can feel the hurt and pain that I feel. Maybe I should file for a divorce and get away from this imposter. If I decided to reconcile with him would I ever be able to trust him again; could I look at him daily and not see his indiscretions in place of his face. What should I do in regards to Felicia; is she a friend or an enemy. Thinking of how to move on from this dark experience, clouds her minds enough to allow her to fall asleep shortly after ten.

Although Brian was told not to return home tonight he decided to disregard the warning and went home after work. When he arrived he was shocked and upset to see that Lisa wasn't home. He had already attempted every way he could think of to contact her but he felt as if he was now option less. Other than if a relative was sick out of town or if she was working on a late night photo shoot, Lisa was always at home awaiting him. This was not a comforting feeling for Brian. Realizing that she probably checked into a hotel for the night to clear her mind he went to bed alone. After an hour of tossing and turning he checked his phone. He scrolled down the contact list and thought about various women and experiences as he scrolled from one name to another. Being well intoxicated and full of pent up emotion and lust Brian was horny as hell with a solid pipe ready to deliver pleasure to whomever was in need. Thinking in the back of his mind how his dick and lustful desires are the reasons he is horny as hell right now, with no one to pleasure, ironically.

Knowing he is being punished for his mistakes he struggles with the thought that tonight he be sexless for the first time in three months. When it came to sex and women he had always been very fortunate. In high school he was a baseball and wrestling star, and in college he became president of his fraternity while just being a sophomore. Over the years he had tasted and swam in quite a few different type of woman. He has had Caucasian, Black, Puerto Rican, Brazilian, German, Russian, Chinese, and so on. Although there are a few types he hadn't had yet, his sexual hit list was well documented and had become advanced and extensive. He was in the process of checking off different situations and types of experiences. He has had threesomes, sex in the club, encounters with swingers and recently sex with a neighbor and so on. He had accomplished so much yet still had a lot more to check off of his sexual hit list. Unfortunately he met a keeper and married her although he wasn't ready to settle down yet. Being selfish he decided to acquire her while the opportunity was at hand. He knew that it was a strong possibility he'd never get to accomplish everything on his hit list but the recognition he receives and the admiration of the young pledges and lower ranking members keeps him feeling relevant.

When Samantha entered the bedroom Troy was awake and watching the ten o'clock news. He asked Samantha how was her day and her face responded with a look that said: how dare you act as if you care about the way my day went; her mouth responded with it was eventful. The tone was one of disgust. He then dared to ask, how is Lisa holding up? Oh, so you knew about it, hmmn, responds Samantha. How do you think she is doing? Her husband and the center of her life has been lying, cheating and making a complete fool of her around town behind her back. I swear if you ever step out on me I better not find out, me or my friends, or you'll pay. You are such a hypocrite Samantha you've told me on several occasions to go and find someone else to fuck. So what that was then this is now and like I said then, don't let no one find out especially me, answered Sam. Troy you just don't understand. I am not a piece of meat or a porn star. My drive for sex is nowhere near as high as yours. You want it four times a day every day. Yep and what's wrong with that, interrupts Troy. I just can't do that Troy, you want way too much. I truly would be comfortable with sex twice, says Samantha. Troy says twice a day would be okay with me. Samantha shook her head no. Troy asked twice a week? She shook her head no again. Troy said: I know you aren't talking about twice a month.

What's wrong with that Troy, at least I'm giving you some sex? You should be happy with whatever amount of sex

I give you. Are you fucking serious asks Troy? How fucking selfish and self-centered can you be, Sam? Here it is, you have a good, loyal, and able man whom which you keep on the shelf. Instead of pleasing me you rather tell me to seek pleasure elsewhere. Yet I have never hit you or hurt you and even though you have given me permission haven't stepped out on you and you won't even try to please me sexually. Troy all you ever want, think and talk about is sex; I'm going to bed Troy. So it is like that Sam; you don't like the conversation so you just gone go to sleep to avoid it, hunh. You need to learn some pointers from your friend, mumbles Troy. I KNOW YOU DIDN'T GO THERE, Troy, yells Samantha. Sam, quiet down please asks Troy. Look here you sexual tyrant. Lisa is willing to do whatever her husband wants sexually yet and still he goes out and sleeps with God knows how many women; so what good does pleasing your man sexually do you?

Samantha that was Brian you know that I'm different, I actually love and care about your emotions and well-being, declares Troy. My every thought and motive in regards to you is to please and pleasure you as well as stimulate you both mentally and physically. The things Brian did to Lisa I would never do to you, we are nothing alike. You both are men; and all men are dogs, replied Samantha. For some reason the male species can't help but to allow the little brain to control the big one. I can't believe you said that Samantha. I honestly hope that you are just speaking out of anger and frustration and not truthfully out of your heart. What do I have to do to prove my devotion Sam? What will it take for you to treat me the way I deserve to be treated? Why do I go above and beyond in my pursuit of keeping you happily pleased when you could care less about how I feel and my concerns? Listen here Troy, goodnight; I have to start my new job tomorrow and I don't have time for this shit tonight. Troy watched Samantha roll over and go to bed. Upset and frustrated Troy descended upon the basement to his normal late night retreat. He cut on some music and began to drink.

New beginnings

Lisa awoke not even an hour after she fell asleep somewhere around eleven thirty. She had a dream that she went home to make up, only to find Brian in the bed that they share with not one but both of the neighbors engaging in sexual activities. Although it was just a dream, it looked as clear as day and the pain felt intensely real. So real she was partially soaked around her neck and chest. She went into the kitchen to get something to drink and heard the music playing gently in the basement. She decided to accompany whoever else was having trouble sleeping. When she went into the basement she discovered Troy alone drinking and ranting to himself. She sat at the bar with him and asked if she could have a drink. Sure Lisa, why not; what'll you be having? I don't mean to be difficult Troy; I'll take whatever you are drinking, answers Lisa. I apologize for the inconvenience I may have caused you tonight.

I was going to go to a hotel but Samantha insisted I stay here. Troy mumbled: I bet she did! Lisa ignored his mumble. She then took her shot of brandy to her mouth and downed it then asked for another. Troy said alright but don't take in too much too quick. Lisa gave Troy what he now realized was the universal: Don't Tell Me What To Do, woman look; then proceeded to down the refill. Troy just watched in amazement. Lisa asked Troy why wasn't he upstairs asleep with his lovely wife. Troy threw back his shot and simply replied can't sleep. Can I ask you a question Troy, said Lisa. If you had a woman that was more than willing to please you in almost any way imaginable, would you jeopardize losing her because someone is flirting with you and giving you compliments? Or better yet, would you sleep with your neighbor knowing your wife is destined to find out?

With all due respect Lisa I do not wish to be in the middle of this dispute between you and dumb dumb. What, asks Lisa? Look here Lisa, if you were my woman I wouldn't ever let another come in between us. Don't tell Brian I said this but, he is a fucking idiot for thinking of sexing someone else let alone actually doing it. From the descriptions of the things you are willing to do to please him sexually; personally I'd live inside you if you were mine. We would sex so often there would be no energy or semen left for me to give away. After seeing the change in facial expression on Lisa's face Troy realized they may be talking inappropriately. Lisa gestured her glass singling for a refill. She then slid Troy a bag of pot and a package of cigars, all of which she relieved from the possession of Brian; she asked could he roll it up for her. He started to ask a question but her facial expression changed shutting him up before he finished. He rolled up for her and in return she smoked with him and left him the remains. She finished her last drink and went back upstairs.

Tim was prepared to make his greatest achievement out of his new job at Companion Life. To his amazement his co-workers were both women and rumored to be highly attractive. Tim was asked to develop a criterion for selecting a sole mate. It was his task to help develop and evaluate a set of general questions that would assist in the development of a profile specifically catered depending upon the response. The company feels that asking a question five different ways can help ensure the honest response was given. Once they have determined the truthful response it helps placing them into categories and making matches based upon the results. Applicants will eventually be asked to answer questions on a scale basis.

For example: How important is communication to you in a relationship; on a scale of one to twenty, with one representing absolutely irrelevant and twenty representing absolutely vital. Based on the answers a detailed profile is developed and then compared to other relevant profiles until a match on over forty characteristics are assessed and attained. It is the company's belief that linking people with like-minded characteristics in some categories is vital to the longevity of the pairing while keeping some differences, allowing for opposites to attract. As the behavioral analysis consultant Tim was tasked to create this group of questioning in order to help determine and assess the value, motives, and expectations of each individual applicant. According to his superiors the marriage counselor is also going to work on a criterion. Tim spent most of Monday night thinking and developing initial questions and reasons explaining how the answer fits into the various categories. His job was to not only evaluate applicants and develop a working model profiling system for matching soul mates, but also to educate the staff as to how and why it works.

Meanwhile in the basement Troy is attempting to drink himself to sleep. It has been over a week since he has had any type of sexual contact with his wife outside of the occasional kiss. To make matters even worse due to Samantha's company being there, he has not been able to relieve himself manually either. The pent up sexual frustration inside him has built up to the point of massive eruption or even paroxysm. Troy attempted to cloud his mind with Brandy but could not stop thinking. Troy could not stop thinking of the different women he has encountered today and the way he had envisioned them naked. With every thought his penis begins to harden. He then thinks about his wife and how she should be the one demanding and influencing his thoughts. How could she be so selfish to have refused him day after day and night after night when she knows how much he needs sex?

He was even more frustrated that tonight they had argued over some bullshit that Brian did. Samantha knew damn well that he was nothing like Brian in regards to his treatment of her; yet she uses that as an excuse to further punish him. Feeling as if the brandy was ineffective, Troy decided to roll up two blunts of pot. He sat behind at the bar and lit up. All he could do was try and ignore the fact that there was not just one beautiful woman asleep upstairs, but there were three. He thought about the women one by one in a very sexual manner; although the separate experiences were exhilarating; when he combined them thinking of him participating in an orgy with all three women at once. Troy could no longer take it and decided that he was a grown man and this was his house, so he put a flick in the DVD player in the basement a begin to watch. For Troy, his preferred type of pornography was that with a storyline. Troy put in a movie titled *Forbidden Encounters*.

The first scene consisted of a woman consoling her sister whose husband has left her for a younger woman. The woman then calls over her boyfriend and allows him to take her sister's mind off of the previous guy. Knowing that two of Samantha's friends were upstairs Troy lowered the television volume to that of a whisper in hopes that they wouldn't hear the porn movie playing. In the back of his mind he fantasized that one of the ladies joined him. Troy leaves the music playing low enough to not disturb anyone upstairs but loud enough to drown out any screams or moans coming from the TV. Troy had watched a good five minutes of the flick before he heard a noise close to him. He turned around and looked but saw nothing or no one. He redirected his attention towards the movie and emergency release of built up semen that he could no longer bear. Troy begins his manual release by pleasuring himself while watching the flick. It's at the moment in the movie where the women were sucking the guy's cock; about to be positioned to get fucked. He heard a moan, but not from the TV. With his penis in hand and erected and the movie clearly playing, he had no way hide or deny his reality. He turned around hoping it was his imagination and no one was there. When he turned he was completely taken back, by the sight of one of Samantha's houseguests; touching herself.

Drunk and home alone still, he questions whether this will become the normal type of night he endures, Brian is distraught. Confused and aggravated that in his most trying time of need his friends did not agree with him, take up for him, or assist him in rectifying the situation. On top of that, his wife didn't come home, which with the exception of when she's working out of town, she never does. The next morning when he awoke, he attempted to contact Lisa but had no luck. Horny from the night before, it was Brian's erection that woke him up this morning and with no Lisa around he put on a movie and handled it himself. Afterwards he showered and relaxed just lying about the condo. He eventually left to go and get some breakfast but was stopped in the hall by Lesley. Although he hadn't had the opportunity to meet her yet he was not disappointed. You must be Brian, I've heard nothing but good things from and about you; I'm Lesley by the way.

I am Kim's partner and she told me that you don't disappoint; so I was wondering, when might I be able to taste that dick? Excuse me, says Brian. Oh, don't act like a bitch, I mean we both like pussy, right! It just so happens that I like both: pussy and dick, good dick that is. So Brian, what do you say? If you want you can have me and Kim at the same time. Your offer is very, very, tempting but I think I'll have to decline. You'll what, says Lesley! What, are you scared of pussy all of a sudden, are chickening out on me? Am I just too much woman to handle? Wait a minute, snaps Brian! As you have already heard and been told pussy doesn't scare me, on the contrary I tame pussy and eat it for breakfast! Don't ever for one second think I'm not man enough to fuck you and put it down at the same time; right now is just not the right time! Well it is morning and I know you find me attractive what's the hold up, says Lesley. My wife, answers Brian if my wife ever found out it would be the end of us. Lesley asked: is your wife home now? He replied no. She followed up with: I won't tell if you won't tell; so let's go back to my place and test you out. I only like to drive vehicles that are luxurious, which I heard you were. So what do you say, me, you and Kim have some fun, maybe re-enact some movies.

The next morning when Karen woke up she immediately took a shower and proceeded to get dressed. By the time she was through, Lisa was in the kitchen drinking coffee while still sobbing and crying. Her face appeared as if she had cried so long she no longer had any tears to cry, rather no fluid came out. Karen asked were you able to get any sleep? Lisa replied not really only a little here and there, how about you? How did you sleep, Karen? Likewise I tossed and turned a little but for the most part I slept okay. Lisa, would you mind dropping me off at my apartment? Sure, I don't mind, answers Lisa. I need to get some fresh air anyway, says Lisa as Troy enters the room heading to the garage ready to leave for work. Good morning ladies, Samantha said she'll be down shortly, you ladies have a great day.

Tuesday morning Tim met up with Troy as usual at the Mean Bean and boy did Troy have a story to tell with regards to Brian. Tim heads toward their normal table to sit with Troy. Tim, come and have a seat, says Troy. I don't know where you were last night and what you were doing but Brian could have used some of your keen words of wisdom. Are you serious or just trying to be funny, asks Tim? No I'm serious says Troy. What did he do now, asks Tim? Was it the neighbor incident again? That's not the half of it, answers Troy. I don't know where to begin. The barbeque was the ignition of the fuse for Brian. So it wasn't the neighbor it was Felicia, the girl from the barbeque, asks Tim. Listen here Tim; to make a long story short, I'll summarize.

While at the barbeque Felicia and Lisa exchanged numbers. What, says Tim? Yes, answers Troy. Supposedly while leaving the party she saw Brian who had successfully avoided her all evening. In return, she called up Lisa and explained it all. No, yelled Tim! Yes, utters Troy! Although I knew that something like this was approaching, I never wanted it to actually happen, proclaims Tim. But I tried to warn him. Tim I haven't told you the whole story yet, says Troy. There's more asks Tim? Yes, replies Troy. After hearing from Felicia's mouth that her and Brian, whom she knew as Ryan was fucking each other; Lisa approached Brian and he basically confessed. He did what, yells Tim! Yep he said he was overwhelmed with guilt and thought he had no other recourse but to come clean.

I can see that happening says Tim. What yells Troy? How could you say that that was the correct thing to do? He was caught so he confessed says Tim. But he fucking confessed to the wrong indiscretion; he confessed to sleeping with the neighbor thinking that Kim was who she had spoken to. Oh, utters Tim. So what happened? As far as I can tell Tim, it might be over for good. Why do you say that Troy. Lisa slept at my house last night answers Troy. Out of the duration of their relationship Lisa has always went home to Brian even when upset. Troy just because she stayed out doesn't mean it is over; it wasn't like she was with another man or anything, replies Tim. Troy had a peculiar look descend upon his face and before Tim could question it, it changed into a seductive smile directed at Daphne their short but very, very attractive waitress.

Short, sexy, and seductive she had a Greek accent and stood somewhere around five feet maybe five feet and one inch tall. She had long semi curly jet black hair with a pair of bluish grey eyes. Petite in physique with very little ass or breast yet what she does have is both intriguing and enticing. She looks at least ten years younger than she is and has the brightest smile. She looks so cute and fragile like you might hurt her during sex; yet when you contemplate it, you just always get the urge to try and knock it out the park. It is something that is just super-duper attractive about a little woman especially one with such a pretty face and beautiful smile, says Troy. If I had just one night with her, I'd show her that I lied and she was the perfect height for me. What are you talking about Troy, asked Tim? One time we were having a conversation and she asked me if I would date a woman her size, being so tall and all?

I thought to myself: ab-so-fucking-lutely especially you, we could do all sorts of types of freaky things like the vertical sixty nine or the bunny hop. Flattered by the inquiry, and attempting to denounce my true feelings; I defensively told her she was too short, for me at least. I explained that my wife was only a few inches shorter than me. Her response was: why didn't you tell me you had a wife? I replied with: my apologies beautiful lady I didn't know you didn't know that I was married. She then reached for my hand, picked it up, examined it, then replied with hmmn, yet you wear no ring. I countered with: I wear my ring when I desire too. My thoughts, actions and presence define my commitment and dedication to my marriage not a ring. She gave me a super seductive smile and said that if I was ever on the market again she'd love to experience feeling love in the manner in which I had described. See Troy, it is comments and flirts like that will have you in Brian's shoes, says Tim. Brian has no respect for women and never has, especially while in college.

Although the kids were still with their grandparents due to the changes going on pertaining to the new job; Samantha drove to work as if she had the kids with her to determine the typical time of travel. She left home at seven fifteen and arrived to work at eight twenty; twenty-five minutes earlier than intended. To her amazement Leslie was awaiting her arrival with a cup of coffee made just the way Samantha likes. Good morning miss boss lady Samantha, here is your coffee, just the way you like it; as well as all the documents you requested have been postured. You have a twelve o'clock brunch with Dean Richards; just a formality for new administrative employees. In the meantime if you need or want anything, just give me a call. Why, thank you Leslie! I don't know what to say but keep up the good work and I appreciate you, already! Samantha went into her office and began to get acclimated.

The first resume she decided to review was Leslie's. According to the credits listed on the document Leslie was phenomenal, her skills were just fantastic. Leslie is definitely going to be a vital asset to her. Leslie was only two years younger than Samantha and was born and raised in Minnesota and had just received her associates in Office and Operations Management from Samantha's alma mater. Similar to Samantha also was her prior retail and telemarketer experience. For a brief moment Samantha thought to herself: I am very impressed, this Leslie is a younger me, maybe I'll take her under my wings. I have the strangest feeling we are going to become best friends. Then she snapped out of her trance and continued learning the paper identity of her new co-workers and subordinates. She knew that like students, employees aren't always truthful in regards to the skills they possess.

Karen asked Lisa along the way home, what are your plans? What will you do today? Karen was concerned for Lisa's state of mind during this stormy emotional time. I'm not sure, answers Lisa. I might just take a trip for a few days. Then address Brian after my photo shoot is completed Sunday. I can't let this betrayal disrupt the progress of my career. I'm not sure if you know but I'm pinup model, sometimes print and photographers have very little patience for models that can't hide their true emotion and display the desired emotion of the photographer. Oh so that's what you do, says Karen! Yes, I am almost finished earning my associate degree in Marketing but I started modeling to help finance my education and after I did a couple print assignments I was offed a contract to become one of the faces of a premium vodka maker and distributer.

Actually that is sort of how I met Brian. Huh!!! I just don't understand. I thought I was doing above and beyond my duties and still I was messed over and mistreated. You know what; I'm glad his true nature was revealed before I gave him children. The marriage alone is something I can put passed me and never have to deal with again. But what about the love, asks Karen? Love! Huh! I fell out of love with him the moment he confessed to cheating on me with the neighbor; confirming my many previous suspicions. I realized about that same instant as he explained why he did it that, the man I love, he simply was not. I realized last night that Brian is not mature nor man enough for me and I can do and deserve much better. Absolutely, agrees Karen!

Suddenly Karen drifts off into her thoughts, mentally repeating "Man ENOUGH" "Deserves MUCH Better"; she sees Troy pinning her down to the pool table and nibbling on her breast through her t-shirt. She can feel her ass pressed against the pool table and his tongue in her mouth. She hears him call her name; Karen, Karen. Karen, Karen we're here. The voice went from Troy's to Lisa's and Karen snapped out of her daydream. Karen, we're here, repeats Lisa. Sorry about that, I must have spaced out says Karen. I didn't get much sleep last night. No worries girl replies Lisa! Hopefully you'll have a little time to take a nap before going to work.

Good morning Tim; hey there Mr. Tall dark and handsome, comments Daphne. What shall you gentlemen have today? I'll have a small cup of jasmine tea says Tim; and for you Troy? Just wrap a bow around your waist with a card that reads: for Troy, and I'll have all I need. Oh Troy, says Daphne while blushing, if circumstances were different I'd take you up on that opportunity. So what on the menu might you fancy today, asks Daphne? Troy smiled and said good to know; I'll have medium coffee and a banana nut muffin, thanks. So Tim, have you heard from Brian today? Not really, other than an odd text about four thirty this morning stating that he hates when I am right and he hopes I find a woman as soon as possible. I just dismissed it as a drunken text or his insensitive way of being funny. I texted him back this morning and asked was he stopping by here this morning but Brian never replied back. I just attributed the lack of a response to him being drunk and probably passed out. I start my new gig today and don't really have time his shenanigans.

Speaking of which, Troy I'll be leaving early this morning, in about ten minutes in order to get to work on time. I have already started the task I've been given and I am enjoying the entire creation process as well as the program development aspect. It is almost like making history. How do you figure asks Troy? It is because the mold, or model, or formula used to successfully match the people, will be of my own creation. It's like putting my rubber stamp of approval on each match made. Not to mention I'm going to be able to finally match myself with the person who could possibly be my best friend and spouse forever. Tim, you seem really eager and anxious to get to work and start, says Troy. Now don't get me wrong I support you and am not trying to be funny but I have a question or two. First of all, is this service available to anyone and everyone or just certain people?

Although you previously mentioned that gender is one of the categories or attributes considered in the determination process; do you take into consideration a person's sexual preference and or orientation? What are you trying to say Troy? Tim, for example: If the questions or rather the responses given say that profiles two and three hundred and two are perfect matches but they are of the same gender. What will that mean Tim, If one of them say, profile two was a heterosexual, does that mean he or she should start searching for partners of their same gender or what? Also, if say, profile four matches up with six other profiles, how would you determine whom is the best match for that person; and how would you prove that the one selected was the best fit out of the six?

On the way to work Karen attempted to analyze herself, trying to determine whether there was a motive for her lust filled sinful dream with a forbidden partner. Even more perplexing was that it felt good to have Troy inside her. When Karen had awoken she was creamy and moist and her panties were soaked; yet she knows in reality she can't stand Troy. Karen arrived to work eager to help use the knowledge she had acquired while away in school. She needed to focus on other people's issues, desires, and intentions and not get hung up on her own. She met with her boss and a Human Resource Manager to finish taking care of any loose ends. Afterwards her supervisor Ms. Franks introduced her to the company and showed Karen her office and gave her a tour of the facility.

Ms. Frank informed Karen that on Friday at eleven there is a logistics brainstorming meeting in the second boardroom. Bring a notepad and a pen and be vocal and insightful during this meeting Karen. It will be led by our behavioral analyst Tim Hillard say Ms. Franks. Karen thought to herself Tim Hillard, hmmn, where have I heard that name before? Karen you will work with him closely and together you will help create the formula on how we evaluate answers given by our clients, says Ms. Franks. When you all are complete we will test it out on ourselves as a control. About twenty minutes after Ms. Franks left Karen's office she had returned and brought along Tim Hillard to introduce the two of them to one another; since they would be required to work hand and hand with each other. Knock! Knock! Excuse me Karen; I would like you to meet Tim. Stunned by her beauty he thinks, she looks even more beautiful in her work attire. Why hello Karen it is a pleasure to meet you officially. Taken back by his handsome appearance in his suit and tie she doubted this was the same Tim she had met just a few days earlier. Hello Tim, how are you doing? I knew I had heard your name before says Karen while blushing.

Do you two know each other asks Ms. Franks? Their facial expressions alone answered her question yet they both verbally admitted to having mutual friends. Ms. Franks was just delighted by the answers and immediately envisions the prospect of Tim and Karen uniting; she saw that the chemistry between the two of them in that instance was love worthy. Being that both Ms. and Mr. Franks met in the workplace and had been together over twenty two years she knew firsthand how long hours of working within close proximity of someone else can form a bond. Also she just so happen to be a hopeless romantic. Ms. Franks uttered interesting! Well it appears that you both are on good terms so working together shouldn't be a problem. It may even help enrich the process and progress since you both already know one another, says Ms. Franks. Well, I'll let you two get started and Tim we are looking forward to your presentation.

Troy had finished teaching both of his morning classes and was about to leave for lunch. He had not spoken to Samantha all day and yet she was just across campus. Troy knew that today was Sam's first day in her new official capacity and that she would be busy. Troy was in deep thought contemplating what he desired to eat when Rebecca approached. As she entered his peripheral vision he instantly acknowledges her by the whipping around of his neck. As the silhouette enlarged and his vision became astute he seductively bit his bottom lip in a lustful demeanor. When he realized it was her and what he was displaying he adjusted. All you have to do is ask for it and it's yours Troy, whispers Rebecca! Good morning beautiful says Troy; what are you going to do if I decide to take you up on that offer? Ask me and find out answers Rebecca. Troy replied I knew you were just talking. Rebecca then stated that she was serious and that she already has an apartment right off campus for them to go to. Troy just say you want me and I drain you completely dry; but I can show you better than I can tell you! Troy replies is that so, are you sure you ready for me to be inside you? Will you be able to keep our professional relationship separate from our extra-curricular relationship? You do realize that this will be just a sexual relationship and I have no intentions of leaving my wife or home? Listen Troy you aren't the only one with attachments and truthfully, I just want to feel your dick inside of me, not make you a baby daddy, says Rebecca. I am an adult and will handle all my affairs ladylike. If you play your role I'll play mine, continues Rebecca. Hmmn.

Okay Rebecca, I want you, I admit it says Troy. I want to undress you, caress you and explore every inch of your of your body with my eyes and hands. I want to travel your body using only my lips and my tongue. I want to nibble on several parts of your body! Hmmn, like where, asks Rebecca? For starters your ears, traveling by way of kisses I'd then move on to your nipples. When I arrive at your clitoris I will twirl my tongue in a counter clock-wise motion around it continuously. Alternating between nibbling gently and delicately sucking while decisively licking you in a region I've only fantasized about thus far. Rebecca could not hold back her lustful intentions and her face displayed a look of pure desire. She was definitely aroused by the description of his intentions and in return wrote down an address on the back of a business card. Rebecca handed Troy the card and said meet me here in ten minutes.

Troy watched in utter amazement as Rebecca walked away. Troy watched her ass twerk up and down, cheek by cheek, left then right; all the while imagining what he is about to do to her. In a moment of devotion Troy calls Samantha to see if she wanted to occupy his time and do lunch; after what transpired last night he would only compile his transgressions. When he calls her, he is informed by Leslie that Samantha said that: if Troy were to call, let him know I'm busy but will talk with him later. Although Troy knew it was officially her first day at her new job and that she might be busy, he felt wronged.

Decisions

Around five o'clock when it was time for the employees to leave for the day Tim was preparing for a late night shift. Tim and Karen decided to work over in order to complete the categorization chart in which the numerous questions asked will be categorized in. The objective is to identify specific values derived from the manner in which a question is asked and then answered. If you are attempting to determine a person's traits and tendencies, asking them similar questions worded differently can yield different even contradicting responses; which in return casts suspicion or supports honesty, building trust levels. Karen didn't mind having to work late especially since it is with Tim. Although he befriended Troy, he was nothing like Troy. She was already attracted to him and now that she knows how intelligent he is she is definitely interested. As for Tim, winning the lottery wouldn't be a comparison to how lucky he feels to be able to work side by side with Karen. If he is truly lucky he'll be able to claim her as his own one day.

For the first time since they first laid eyes upon one another Tim and Karen were face to face and alone. Although in a professional atmosphere the attraction between and for one another is more transparent then air. Karen asked Tim, so how should we begin? Tim took a deep breathe then exhaled and exalted out an amorous smile. Karen asked was everything alright? Tim replied, honestly I think that you are beautiful and I am attracted to you in more ways than one; but while at work I'll keep it professional. Tim observed Karen blushing at his statements so he continued. Unless you tell me now there isn't a chance in hell of us getting together, I think I'd be an absolute fool to not try and acquire you. He noticed she was no longer blushing nor smiling so he shut up. Now that I have that off my chest, back to work says Tim.

My whole purpose is to clearly define the intended results we are looking for. As well as explain the steps we will take to acquire the information needed. I will explain why this method works and the mechanics behind it. Also we will be teaching them how to assess the data received and make correct interpretations. You will help me develop the questions that should evoke the most honest response. Karen was only half way listening to Tim; she could not stop herself from imagining this intelligent, handsome man in front of her, inside of her. Tim asked her, do you think you can handle what I need you to do? Karen heard, in the most seductive male voice known, do you think you can handle me inside of you? She moaned out, yyeeesss! Tim immediately looked into her eyes and asked, are… you alright? She did a quick shiver and answered in a normal tone, yes, I can work with you on that. You are actually quite brilliant Tim. Tim smiled looking at her in her face and in return she smiled and blushed revealing her dimples.

So… Karen I need to test you out first, I mean test it out on you first! I mean… What type of characteristics do you look for in a mate? Okay, that's a good question responds Karen. Uh um! I actually need you to answer the questions Karen, say Tim. Truthfully, he adds! Alright, Alright, I'll answer. When I look for a companion I look for strength, good looks, financial stability, intellectual capacity, and a genuine personality. What characteristics do you feel your perfect mate should possess, asks Tim? He should be: loving, caring, trustworthy, successful, generous, handsome, devoted, mature, and well equipped in the bed! Hmmn, mumbles Tim! What characteristics do you feel are the most vital to a successful relationship? Karen answered questions and defined words, terms and feelings for over an hour. Unknowingly, she revealed enough detailed information about herself to Tim that he has more than enough data to develop a working profile on her. She then looked at him and said: your turn!

Brian was in a terrible place with a defining decision at hand. How often does an attractive woman walk up to you a say that she wants you to screw her and her girlfriend. He knows that this is something that he probably will never get offered again. Although, he has had a threesome before; this time he was more experienced and had some untried positions previously unknown to him at time of previous threesome. On the other hand he was already in trouble with his wife who is probably considering divorce right as he thinks. Brian thinks to himself, maybe I should pass and go find Lisa. Then again Kim never told on him, which means that they may be trustworthy; beside I'm horny as hell and there are two pussies being offered, one new to me. Not to mention what if Lisa doesn't come home, now you'd have the next best thing to in-house pussy; next-door pussy.

So Brian, are you saying you don't want some of this, asked Lesley while reaching inside her shirt and pulling out one of her breast. Brian couldn't help himself he bit his bottom lip and his penis began to grow. Upon seeing his response through his body language Lesley reached into her panties and began to finger herself in front of Brian. Lisa was no longer on his mind and he was losing decision making power to the will of his smaller head. He reached down and grabbed his dick assessing its hardness and while simultaneously alerting her to his rising star. She then took out her finger and put it in his mouth; then asked how do I taste? Brian completely under a spell of lust sucked on her finger; attempting to taste any, and all the juices from her vagina that transferred onto her finger. His response was delicious let's do this. He leaned in to kiss her but she backed away and said she only kisses women not men. Don't get me wrong I will suck the skin off your dick but we will never connect tongues. For real, it's like that Lesley. Hey, I like what I like she replied. The only part of you that will enter my mouth is your penis; and if you must use your tongue, you can eat me out but I mainly want your dick inside my three holes.

Troy makes it to the destination written on the back of the business card and thought about last night. Troy had what he could only describe as ironic chaos and the events of today are following suite. It all started when Brian screwed over his wife Lisa who used my wife Sam for a crutch which led to Sam fucking me over sending me away again sexually frustrated. Ironically Brian's unappreciated wife ended up alone with Sam's sexually deprived husband. Although they have never been attracted to one another both are under intense emotional distress, which could be why a line was crossed that should have never. Troy thinks back upon last night in his basement.

After drinking a lot of liquor and smoking some grass, Troy decided that he could no longer contain his pinned up sexual frustrations and decided to relieve himself manually. While in the process of doing just that he was interrupted and discovered by one of his wife's houseguests. After hearing a noise behind him he looked to see if someone was behind him and there was. When he saw her he jumped up and then unsuccessfully tried to put away his penis which was erected to a length of seven inches or longer. She said it is okay I won't tell anyone and don't stop because of me. I promise I won't tell Sam a thing as a matter of fact may I join you. Join me says Troy. I don't mean that, I mean that I'm used to sex every night and I too need to release. If you don't share any details I won't either she says. She then pushes him back on the couch a presses play on the remote control then sat next to him.

She opened her robe and began to finger herself. Troy was confused and in a state of denial which quickly turned to lust. While watching the movie and hearing her moan gracefully in his ear, his penis became stiff and started to flinch back and forth. She looked down at his long thick and pretty dick and thought to herself, damn Sam is a lucky woman to have that dick every day. After while she places her hand on the shaft of his penis initiating a stiff flinch which she grab tight and held. She asked him why he isn't fucking his wife. His reply was if I could I would. When was the last time, she asked? His reply was way too long. She licked her lips and slowly began to stroke his penis up and down with her hands. She could feel the smooth yet textured skin on his penis and the stiffness within it. She thought it looked aesthetically pleasing and took notice that it was of a two tone color pallet.

She noticed that his blood vein on top of his penis was thick and ran in a straight line from the base until the separation line that divided the two shades of brown. As soon as it crosses over to the lighter brown region which houses his head; then the vein takes a sharp left turn then curves back towards the tip of his penis. The head on Troy's penis looked big and clearly defined like the mane of a lion. As she caresses his penis all he could do was fall into a state of relaxation. Instinctively he extended his arm around her back. Feeling the appreciation Troy has just for her touching his dick, she motions to put his dick in her mouth but stops directly above it. He whispers please continue. She then releases slob and spit from her mouth and allows it to drip down Troy's penis. She quickly wraps her lips around the head of his penis and begins to blow and twirl her tongue around it.

Suddenly Troy stops day dreaming and pays close attention to the vehicle approaching his. The car parks and the lovely Miss Rebecca exits the vehicle and waves for him to follow her inside. Troy hesitated, thinking about how Samantha might feel but quickly realized that Samantha obviously doesn't care how he feels; which is fueling the reasoning that led him here, today. Troy proceeded to follow Rebecca into the building where he planned on living and acting out a desire he has had since he started working here. Once inside Rebecca instantly pounced on Troy, giving him kisses and taking cheap feels of his goods. Troy embraced the opportunity to fulfill his desire to undress and caress Rebecca. Adding to the spice of lust was that he was going to get paid for this since he technically was still on the clock.

He enjoyed the way her lips felt on his own and now knew what her nibbling on his neck really felt like. He took his share of cheap feels during the process of him undressing her. Although Troy had seen several vagina's before, it was something mesmerizing about the way Rebecca's vagina looked. It was pleasantly plump and looked so juicy and enticing to him. Not completely shaven but the design left was lined up as if professionally sculptured. Shining through her lace underwear was her clitoris piercing which when touched by anything, sent pleasure vibrations coursing through her body. Troy was ready to eat and for once he actually had a full course meal standing right in front of him. He then began to give Rebecca what she wanted and receive exactly what he has been missing. They were the perfect complement to each other; her pussy was so warm and moist and his dick was so big and hard they both felt as if their wishes and erotic desires had come true.

Lisa called up her sister and let her in on the current status of her and Brian's relationship. Her sister stays right outside of Chicago Illinois which is where Lisa plans on heading in an attempt to try and clear her mind. Although Lisa and Brian have some history she feels at this point the union between her and Brian is history. For Lisa, trust and communication are the most important and vital tools needed to produce and maintain a successful and healthy relationship. Now that Brian has given her absolute confirmation that he cannot be trusted, she refuses to accept his less than desirable, deceitful, disrespectful behavior. Not even if they were just dating would she be okay with her mate sexing the world; let alone that type of reckless behavior from her husband. It had been a long time since someone had made her feel insignificant or as if she wasn't worthy of being the main woman. Her insecurity didn't flow to the surface often but this time it had spilled over and ran like a waterfall.

Never before did she feel so unattractive or unwanted. She questioned whether she could've done more to or for Brian to make him want to stay home. She wondered if she just didn't have what it takes to keep a man faithful and dedicated. Then Lisa realized that again, she was excusing Brian's wrong doings and trying to justify his actions due to a lack of her actions. She didn't want to believe that another woman could disrupt her life so easily. How could she love someone who apparently didn't feel the same as her and would throw it all away for a stranger? The more she thought about it the less value and worth she felt she deserved. A good man is devoted to his wife and tends to do whatever it takes to please his woman; yet in Brian's case it feels as if he is constantly trying to define his boundaries within the several grey areas of life.

Tim checked his watch and suggested that he give his responses tomorrow due to the volume of data that would be generated and the time needed to collect it. Karen said absolutely not, you'll do them today. I don't mind working over. So Tim, what type of characteristics do you look for in a mate? Tim proceeded to answer every question honestly and with pride. While every question was asked and answered, Tim paid very close attention to Karen's facial expressions and body language. After an hour or so, Karen now had raw data that when interpreted would reveal the inner working of Tim. Tim said: I think we've captured enough data for today. Let's call it a night and go at it again in the morning. Is that alright with you? Are you satisfied? Yes that's okay with me, answers Karen. We can finish where we left off at today, tomorrow. Are you hungry Karen I know a place nearby? Tim, I don't think that would be wise. I mean we work together. Hmmn, so you do like me, mumbles Tim.

What, no I didn't mean it like that, says Karen? Just admit it Karen. We are grown and I don't kiss and tell so admit it. Listen I'll admit that your method for extracting information is quite brilliant. Okay I guess I'll accept that, says Tim. You do have some qualities I like in a man but we could ruin too much if we hooked up but didn't work out. Tim says alright now, I can accept that for an answer; but know this. If you ever decide to let me into your life, I promise you more good times than you have ever experienced. I would do everything possible to make sure you keep: a smile on your face, butterflies in your stomach, a glow that everyone else can clearly see, and you moist enough to feel as if you have a sea between your knees. I don't mean to be blunt but, you are far too good of a catch to throw back in the sea, regardless of how many fish are in there. But seriously, let's get something to eat asks Tim. Just a meal, no marriage, it doesn't have to be a date; we don't have to have sex, or even a kiss; unless you want too. What, says Karen! Just dinner no strings attached says Tim. So how about it Karen! Alright Tim, let's do it!

Samantha had meetings for most of the morning and afternoon. For lunch Samantha took Leslie up on her suggestion to bring Sam some steak and lobster back from the Captain's Lobster Trap. Once all the meetings were over, Samantha asked Leslie did she have any messages for her. When Samantha looked through the messages she noticed that Felicia had called twice and left a message each time. Samantha decided to call Felicia back and setup a place to meet after work tonight. Samantha had always appreciated the kindness and consideration Felicia always showed her and felt there was no reason to alienate Felicia, especially when she knew firsthand that Brian was a dog. She agreed to meet up with Felicia and discuss the events of last weekend and yesterday. Samantha decided that she would still maintain the friendship between herself and Lisa as well as the friendship between herself and Felicia. Next Samantha sent Troy a text message informing him that she would be home late and that she would eat while out.

Felicia was relieved to still have Samantha to talk to and spend time with. Working together for so long had made them become close friends and now that they are no longer working together, Felicia is happy to still be able to continue their friendship. Felicia was the first to arrive at the restaurant and picked out a booth for them to sit at. She ordered a bottle red wine, a brand they both enjoyed then she ordered some appetizers and bread. Samantha arrived shortly afterwards and she immediately hugged her friend and gave her comfort, then they sat down. The waiter showed up with their bottle of wine and asked if they were ready to order. The women said that they needed some time and he should check back after the appetizers have come. The waiter replied: whatever you beautiful ladies desire, I'm your man, let me know and I'll make it happen; whatever you desire. I'll just be over there waiting for you. As the waiter walked away Felicia began to vent.

Huh, why are all men such fucking flirts? How are we expected to trust men when the greater majority of them are simply incapable of trusting or not lusting, says Felicia? Samantha says there are some good men out there but it usually takes a woman to mold her man into a good man. Most men aren't incapable of trust; they just possess so many negative traits and tendencies. Without positive reinforcement and redirection from a strong woman, those traits and tendencies will turn into personality and demeanor says Samantha. It took me forever to mold Troy into the man I wanted him to be and yet still over ten years later I still have more work to do. Well Sam, I just want someone who I can emotionally connect with and I'm not sure if I can find that in a grown man; and I don't want a boy. Both women snickered. Then Samantha asked, are you saying you're considering a woman?

Felicia answered yes, I guess I am. Maybe it would be easier to connect emotionally; have you ever considered it Sam. Considered what answered Sam; being with a woman. Yes replied Felicia, so have you ever thought about it. I'm ashamed to say that I have, and it was recently, admits Samantha. What, yells Felicia. I thought you and Troy were perfect and on equal yet good terms. We are to some extent, it's just… he demands sex too much for me. To be honest I no longer have a desire for sex at all, says Samantha. At all says Felicia. At all answers Samantha, I don't want to give it nor receive it. I've come to the conclusion that I'm at a point in my life where sex is not a want of mine nor desire let alone a necessity, says Samantha. How does Troy feel about that, asks Felicia? Although the look on Samantha's face pretty much answered the question. She verbally admitted he doesn't know yet, I already know he can't go without it. So what will you do Sam, I don't know Felicia.

Reflections

After dropping off Karen, Lisa proceeded to the airport. When Lisa arrived at Minneapolis St. Paul International Airport she purchased her plane ticket. She went and ate breakfast while awaiting the arrival of her departure time. She thought feverishly about the last 24 hours and was filled with mixed emotions. She felt guilt for betraying the relationship that she and Samantha had developed. As for her no good, two timing, excuse of a husband guilt was far from her mind and her heart. She knew that this was a critical moment in her life. That fact that she wasn't a gambling woman helped make her decision a lot easier.

If she forgives him and stays; she would be devaluing the punishment. How could she ever believe that he is incapable of betraying her when he did it so easily and sloppily? People do make mistakes, which is why we apply the 3 strikes you're out rule. Though, some mistakes are heinous enough to receive maximum punishment, regardless of the amount of times committed. What Brian has done to me is severe enough that I divorce him and move on. Had Felicia never come clean I'd still be looking stupid while thinking life is perfect. Even though Brian doesn't deserve a second chance let me talk to him at least once before I leave. She called Brian and received no response. She thought to herself; what now, why is he not answering when all night he was calling me! When his shrug voicemail came on she got upset and left him an emotional message.

As Tim and Karen rode the elevator together down to the parking garage there was a strange silence as both contemplated the outcome of the next two hours. Could there be an outcome that leads to a happy ending thinks Karen? How do I keep it professional when I desire her on a level that is truly personal, thinks Tim? So Karen, should we ride together or take separate cars. I think we should definitely drive in separate vehicles. I don't think it would look good us carpooling on the first day of working together. It's is not like we just met Karen but I'm okay with it, however or whatever you want ; I'm just ready to eat!

Unable to resist the temptation presented to him, Brian engaged in sexual acts with both Kim and Lesley at the same time. Completely engulfed in the sex, Brian ignored his phone when it rang. With two beautiful, super sexy and vivacious women just throwing themselves at him; he was distracted. With no response from her soon to be ex-husband; Lisa left a message saying: *Brian I am going to see my sister and won't be back until Monday. That's if I decide to come back at all. Goodbye. What you have done and been doing is unacceptable and has truly hurt me bad. I'm hurting so bad I don't want to even gaze upon your face; when a few days ago it was what I looked forward too. Please know that I did Love you.* Not realizing the amount of irreparable damage he caused by not answering this particular call. He continued living out a fantasy while simultaneously earning a few more checks on his hit list.

He performed and showed out for both Kim and Lesley. He felt as if he had something to prove to Lesley and wanted Kim to want him routinely. He kept up his performance long enough to ensure that both women were thoroughly satisfied. Although he never intended on being inside their condo at all, he was busy having so much fun that three hours had come and gone. By the time he left the neighbor's house his phone was dead and although he was no longer horny, he was still hungry. It was almost time for him to go to work so he went back home to prepare. After showering and getting dressed he powered up his phone and was reminded about the message that awaited him. He proceeded to listen to the message not realizing the severity of it.

After listening to the message in its entirety Brian was in disbelief and replayed it several more times. After realizing what was said he immediately called Lisa to talk to her. Being in mid-flight Lisa's phone went straight to voicemail which he noticed had been changed. Instead of hearing her voice and the normal message she had recorded, he heard a computer generated voice saying leave a message for 612 555 9433. He listened to her message one more time and then contemplated what his next steps should be. He texted Craige and told him that he needed to talk to him. I need you to connect me with your jeweler or lawyer, maybe even both.

After Troy's fantasy driven lunch time adventure inside Rebecca's play land; Troy returned to work as if nothing had happened. He felt invigorated and revitalized! The last 24 hours has been totally foreign and spontaneous to him. He knows his new behavior is absolutely out of character. Yet still he wants more. He thinks to himself: If only my wife could enjoy sex like I do; I could live out fantasies with and inside her, instead of in my mind or with someone else. Who can I talk to? Who can help me make sense out of all this? Why do I not feel wrong for doing what I know is wrong? If I can make peace with myself and she never find out, did I do any wrong? Does the permission from my wife to find someone who is willing to do the sexual acts that she won't; justify my not feeling guilty? Or am I falling out of love and just don't care anymore?

Troy called Craige and asked if he would swing by Brian's bar tonight. He said that he needed some advice. Craige said I'll be there until 6 but after that he had to meet up with Penelope. Craige asked was everything okay? Troy replied yeah but maybe it's too okay! Craige said are you sure I'm the one to help you. This sounds like it is more up Tim's alley but whatever; I'll be there. Tim started his new job today and I haven't talked to him since this morning, replied Troy.

I don't want to leave nor loose Troy but we are just no longer on the same page with our desires and wants. When he finds out, it'll be either death or divorce. Would it be wrong of me to lead Troy on knowing that this is strongly how I feel and that for him sex is not optional it is a requirement? I mean I know him and he knows me, we understand each other and the reasons why we do the things we do. We are so in tune with each other we can finish one another's statements. I don't want to lose the time and effort that I have invested into making Troy the great man that everyone else see's. Wait Sam, are you telling me that you and Troy are no longer sexually active any more. Look Felicia, I am a career woman who works and has worked extremely hard to get in the position I have acquired. I have a multitude of responsibilities at work that require massive amounts of my energy. Then when I get home I still have the duties of being a mother as well as having to clean up the house. Most days I am just physically drained and mentally exhausted. Then here comes Troy acting like a hungry wolf looking me over like I'm his meal for the night.

The look in his eyes usually erases any thoughts or desires of sex that I had. Girl that is understandable so long as it's not every day says Felicia. It's like whenever I give in it's never enough for him, he's just insatiable. Do you guys have four-play, asks Felicia? I hate to give him oral, he takes forever to cum, replies Samantha. At one point in time I didn't mind sex and four-play but Troy's insatiable appetite burned me out and I no longer have any craving or urges for sex. Don't get me wrong, my husband is excellent in that department but still I have no desire for sex. Aren't you afraid that he'll cheat on you, asks Felicia? Honestly, if it was just sex I probably wouldn't get mad unless it was someone I knew, answers Samantha. Other than sex I couldn't name a problem Troy and I have.

Maybe it is just a phase that you are going through says Felicia. I'm not so sure I think it's much more says Samantha. In my heart I truly do love Troy and everything about him; but deep inside I feel as if we are growing apart instead of closer. I feel the only way to work it out is to attempt and make either Troy or myself change one of our major personality traits. His desire for sex has done nothing but escalate over the years while my sex drive has dissipated. I want with all my heart to grow old with Troy but I know being sexless will be the final straw for Troy; just the mere thought of it he'd shout was fucking unacceptable. I'm so confused; I just don't know what to do cries Samantha. Don't cry Sam; I'm certain you'll figure out what's best for you and get past this situation. Have you asked Karen what you should do? I don't know if I want her to know so much about me and Troy and the way we are intimately. The more details you know about someone the more you tend to cast judgment, we are already so close. Not to mention that her and Troy never really got along.

Despite riding in separate cars to the restaurant both Karen and Tim arrived together. The restaurant was a Mediterranean themed bistro that typically serviced the working crowd during brunch, happy hour, and after work. Tim and Karen were both very inquisitive people and couldn't help but continue processing the raw data learned about one another. Tim asked Karen how is it that she is single? He complimented her on her looks, her intelligence, and what he has seen so far of her personality. She replied, I should be asking the same of you. How about this Karen: I'll answer every question honestly that you ask me if you answer a few for me. Alright Tim, I am game. And so began the unofficial first date between Karen and Tim.

THE

END

Printed in the United States
By Bookmasters